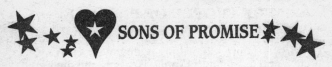

SONS OF PROMISE

'MIDNIGHT SONS and the men of Alaska started all this craziness, but the men of Promise refuse to be outdone. They're just as stubborn, just as ornery, just as proud. And just as lovable. Come to Promise—if you're like me, you'll never want to leave!'

Enjoy

Debbie Macomber

Debbie loves to hear from her readers. You can reach her at P.O. Box 1458, Port Orchard, Washington 98366 USA.

WATCH OUT FOR MORE STORIES FROM PROMISE!

Caroline's Child

Dr. Texas

Nell's Cowboy

Lone Star Baby

THE PEOPLE OF PROMISE:
CAST OF CHARACTERS

Nell Bishop: thirty-something widow with a son, Jeremy, and a daughter, Emma. Her husband died in a tractor accident.

Ruth Bishop: Nell's mother-in-law. Lives with Nell and her two children.

Dovie Boyd: runs an antiques shop and has dated Sheriff Frank Hennessey for ten years.

Caroline Daniels: postmistress of Promise.

Maggie Daniels: Caroline's five-year-old daughter.

Dr. Jane Dickinson: new doctor in Promise.

Ellie Frasier: owner of Frasier's Feed Store.

Frank Hennessey: local sheriff.

Max Jordan: owner of Jordan's Towne & Country.

Wade McMillen: preacher of Promise Christian Church.

Edwina and Lily Moorhouse: sisters. Retired schoolteachers.

Cal and Glen Patterson: local ranchers. Brothers.

Phil and Mary Patterson: parents of Cal and Glen. Operate a local B&B.

Louise Powell: town gossip.

Wiley Rogers: sixty-year-old foreman at the Weston ranch.

Laredo Smith: wrangler hired by Savannah Weston.

Barbara and Melvin Weston: mother and father to Savannah, Grady and Richard. The Westons died six years ago.

Richard Weston: youngest of the Weston siblings.

Savannah Weston: Grady and Richard's sister.

Grady Weston: oldest of the Weston siblings.

Chapter One

A month ago this had been her family home.

Ellie Frasier stood on the tree-lined sidewalk in Promise, Texas, staring up at the traditional two-story house with its white picket fence. The Sold sign stared back at her, telling her that nothing would ever be the same again. Her father was dead, and her mother gone.

This was the house where she'd been born and raised. Where she'd raced across the front lawn, climbed the pecan tree and hung upside down from its branches. On that very porch she'd been kissed for the first time.

Oh, how she'd miss that porch. Countless pictures had been taken of her on these steps. Her mother holding an infant Ellie in her arms the day she brought her home from the hospital in Brewster. Every Easter in a frilly new dress and every Halloween in a costume her mother had sewn for her.

The day Ellie turned thirteen and wore panty hose for the first time, her dad had insisted she have her picture taken on the porch. Then at eighteen, when she was a rodeo princess for the Brewster Labor Day Festival, her father had posed her on the front steps again. At the time he'd told her he'd be taking her picture there in her wedding dress before she left for the church.

Only, her father would never escort her down the aisle.

The rush of pain came as no surprise. She'd been dealing with it for weeks now. And before that, too, while he was in the hospital, desperately ill. But Ellie couldn't believe he would actually die; death was something that happened to other people's fathers, not her own. Not yet. He was too young, too vital, too *special,* and because she'd refused to accept the inevitable, his passing had hit her hard, throwing her emotionally off balance.

Even then, she'd been forced to hold her grief inside. Her mother had needed her to be strong. Ellie's personality was like her father's—forceful, independent and stubborn. Her mother, on the other hand, was fragile and rather impractical, relying on her husband to look after things. She'd been unable to deal with the funeral arrangements or any of the other tasks that accompany death, so they'd fallen on Ellie's shoulders.

The weeks that followed were like an earthquake, and the aftershocks continued to jolt Ellie, often when she least expected it.

Her mother had given her the worst shock. Within a week of the burial service, Pam Frasier announced she was moving to Chicago to live with her sister. Almost immediately the only home Ellie had ever known was put up for sale. By the end of the first week they'd had an offer.

Once the deal was finalized, her mother packed up all her belongings, hired a moving company, and before Ellie could fully appreciate what was happening, she was gone. Whatever she'd left behind, Pam told her daughter, was Ellie's to keep. The family business, too. Pam wanted nothing from the feed store. John had always intended it to go to Ellie.

Squaring her shoulders, Ellie realized there was no use delaying the inevitable. The key seemed to burn her hand as she approached the house for the last time and walked slowly up the five wooden steps. She stood there for a moment, then forced herself to unlock the front door.

A large stack of boxes awaited her. Ellie had a fair idea of what was inside. Memories. Years and years of memories.

No point in worrying about it now. Once she'd loaded everything up and carted it to her rented house, she had to get to the feed store. While her customers had been understanding, she couldn't expect unlimited patience. George Tucker, her assistant—he'd been her father's assistant, too—was trustworthy and reliable. But responsibility for Frasier Feed was Ellie's, and she couldn't forget that.

Which meant she couldn't take the time to grieve properly. Not when she was short-staffed during the busiest season of the year. June brought with it a flurry of activity on the neighboring cattle ranches, and many of those ranchers would be looking to her for their feed and supplies.

By the third trip out to her truck Ellie regretted turning down Glen's offer of help. Glen Patterson was quite possibly the best friend she'd ever had. Although she'd always known who Glen was—in a town the size of Promise, everyone knew everyone else, at least by sight—there was just enough difference in their ages to keep them in separate social circles during their school years.

The Pattersons had been buying their feed from Frasier's for years. Her father and Glen's dad had played high school football together. For the past few years Glen had been the one coming to town for supplies. When Ellie began to work full-time with her dad, she'd quickly developed a chatty teasing relationship with Glen.

She was lighthearted and quick-witted, and Glen shared her sense of humor. Before long she'd found herself looking forward to their verbal exchanges. These days whenever he stopped by, Ellie joined him for a cup of coffee. They usually sat on the bench in front of her store, idling away fifteen or twenty minutes, depending on how busy she was. When the weather discouraged outdoor breaks, they sat in her office to enjoy a few minutes' respite.

It got to be that they could talk about anything. She appreciated his wry good sense, his down-to-earth approach to life. Ellie tended to obsess about problems, but Glen took them in stride. While she ranted and raved, he'd lean his chair against the building wall and tuck his hands behind his head, quietly listening. Then he'd point out some error in her thinking, some incorrect assumption or faulty conclusion. Generally he was right. His favorite expression was, "Don't confuse activity with progress." She could almost hear him saying it now.

It'd been a week or more since his last visit, and Ellie missed him. She could count on Glen to distract her, make her smile. Perhaps even ease this gnawing pain. But when he'd offered to help her sort through the boxes, she'd declined, moving everything on her own. Knowing she'd have to face these memories sooner or later and preferring to do it alone.

Within minutes of her arrival at the feed store, the place was bustling. Naturally she was grateful for the business, but she would have liked a few moments to herself. Then again, perhaps it was best to be hurled into the thick of things, with no chance to dwell on her grief and all the changes taking place in her life.

It was almost two before Ellie could dash into her office for ten minutes, to collect her thoughts and have lunch. Although her appetite was nonexistent, she forced herself to eat half a sandwich and an apple. At her desk, she sifted through the phone messages and found one from Glen. It was unusual for him to call during the day, especially in early summer when he spent most of his time working with the herd. Just knowing she'd been in his thoughts buoyed her spirits.

Since his parents had moved into town and opened the local bed-and-breakfast, Glen and his older brother, Cal, had taken over management of the ranch. Thus far they'd kept the spread operating in the black, doing whatever work they could themselves and hiring seasonal help when necessary. In the last few years, they'd begun cross-breeding their cattle with Grady Weston's stock.

The phone rang and, thinking it might be Glen, Ellie reached eagerly for the receiver. "Frasier Feed."

"Ellie, I'm glad you answered. It's Richard Weston."

If it couldn't be Glen, then Ellie felt pleased it was Richard. He'd recently returned to Promise after a six-year absence, and they'd gone out on a couple of dates before her father's condition worsened.

"How are you?" Richard asked in a concerned voice.

"Fine," she responded automatically, which was easier than confessing the truth. She just couldn't talk about her grief, her deep sense of loss. Maybe Glen was the only person she could share that with, Ellie reflected. But not yet. It was too soon. For now, she needed to forge ahead and do what was necessary to get through the day.

"You've been on my mind a lot the last couple of weeks."

"I appreciate your thoughtfulness, Richard, I really do." Ellie was sincere about that. She'd been a schoolgirl when he left Promise, and like every other female in her class she'd had a major crush on him. Richard was still the best-looking man in town. The years away had refined his features, and he was suave in ways ranchers could never be. City-suave. She liked him well enough but didn't expect anything from their friendship. To be frank, she was flattered that he sought her out. The huge flower arrangement he'd sent for her father's funeral had touched her, it was the largest one there and stood out among the other smaller arrangements. A number of the townsfolk had commented on it.

"I received the thank-you card," he said. "The flowers were the least I could do."

"I wanted you to know how much Mom and I appreciated it." She paused. "It was nice of you to do that for us."

"I'd like to do more, if you'd let me," he said, softly. "If there's anything you need, make sure you phone."

"I will." But it was unlikely she'd take him up on his offer. Not even Glen, her best friend, knew how emotionally shaky she was. The pain was still so new, so raw, that she had to deal with it herself before she could lean on anyone else. Her father had been like that, too, and she was, after all, her father's daughter.

"You know, Ellie," Richard said next, "I think it'd do you a world of good to get out."

A date? Now? No way. Ellie wasn't ready, and besides, she had a million things to do before she gave a thought to her social life. She was about to tell him that when he spoke again.

"Nell Bishop called to tell us she's having a birthday bash for Ruth this Friday night. Sounds like she's going all out. How would you feel about tagging along with me?"

Ellie hesitated.

"You need to relax a little. Have a few laughs," he added with the same empathy he'd shown earlier. "Let me help you through this."

Ellie had received an invitation herself. Attending a party was the last thing she felt like doing, but Nell was a good friend and a good customer. She needed to make at least a token appearance.

"I probably won't stay long," she qualified, thinking it would be best if Richard went without her. They could meet there.

"No problem," Richard quickly assured her. "I'm not much into this birthday thing myself. The only reason I told Nell I'd come was so I could ask you."

"Oh, Richard, that's so sweet."

"Hey, that's just the kind of guy I am."

"If you're sure you don't mind leaving early, I'd be happy to go with you." Ellie had always been fond of Ruth Bishop. She knew that Ruth and Nell had supported each other through the trauma of Jake's death. Nell had lost the love of her life; Ruth had lost her son. Nell had struggled to hold on to the ranch despite numerous hardships, financial and otherwise. Ruth had been a wonderful help, and Ellie was sure Nell had planned this party as a means of thanking her mother-in-law.

"I'll swing by your place around six," Richard suggested.

"Six would be perfect." They chatted a couple of minutes longer, and as she hung up the phone, Ellie realized she was actually looking forward to an evening out. It would feel good to laugh again, and Richard was always entertaining.

THE SUN BEAT DOWN on Glen Patterson. He and his brother were on horseback, driving almost four hundred head of cattle to one of the far pastures. With two hired hands, seasonal help, they'd shuffled all the cattle through narrow chutes, vaccinating them.

Removing his Stetson, he wiped his brow, then glanced quickly at his watch. Ellie had been in his thoughts most of the day. He shouldn't have listened to her protests; he should've stopped at her parents' house that morning despite everything. Ellie could use a helping hand, whether she was willing to admit it or not. The woman was just too damn stubborn.

In his view she'd declined his offer mostly out of pride.

He wondered if she felt mourning should be done in private, and he wanted to tell her she didn't have to hide her grief, that it was okay to accept an offer of help. She didn't have to do everything herself. He knew it had all been a brave front, but he didn't have much choice other than to accept her decision.

Vaccinating the herd was not Glen's favorite task. Still, it was better than checking the cows and heifers for signs of pregnancy, although he strongly suspected the animals weren't any keener on the practice than he was himself. Glen wished to hell someone would invent a urine test for cows.

"I think I'll head on back," Glen told his brother. They'd reached the pasture, and the cattle began to spread out.

Cal's attention didn't waver from the last stragglers. "Going into town?" he asked.

Glen raised his hat a bit. "I was thinking about it," he said with some reluctance. His brother's ability to read his mind was uncanny at times. And damned irritating.

A telltale quiver at the edges of Cal's mouth signaled the beginnings of a smile. "You're going off to see Ellie, right?"

"So what?" Glen didn't care for that tone of voice. His brother never had understood how he and Ellie could be friends and nothing else. But then, Cal had an attitude when it came to women, no matter who they were. Not that Glen blamed him. If a woman had publically humiliated *him* the way Jennifer Healy had humiliated his brother, Glen supposed his own feelings toward the opposite sex would be tainted, too. At times, however, Cal's lack of perspective annoyed him.

"You two should own up to a few truths," Cal announced, as though being two years older gave him some kind of wisdom—or authority.

"Truths?"

"You and Ellie have something going."

"You're right," Glen admitted, and he could see that agreeing with Cal had taken his brother aback. "We're friends. Is that so difficult to understand?" Glen couldn't figure out what it was with his brother, and a few others, too. Even Grady Weston, his lifelong friend and fellow rancher, obviously believed there was more between him and Ellie than friendship.

The fact was that in four years they'd never so much as held hands—which should say something. He simply enjoyed Ellie's company, and she enjoyed his. Anything romantic would ruin one of the best damn friendships he'd ever had. Ellie felt the same way. Okay, so they'd never openly discussed it, but then there was no reason they should. They understood each other. An unspoken agreement.

Yes, that was it; he felt better for having analyzed the situation. "Ellie and I have an understanding," he explained with a sense of satisfaction. Cal wouldn't argue with that. "It's like the way you and I never talk about Bitter End."

Cal's eyes narrowed. Only a small number of families in Promise knew about the ghost town hidden in the Texas hills. Few ever mentioned it. Once, as teenagers, Grady, Cal and Glen had decided to look for the town themselves. It was supposed to be a summertime adventure. Something they could brag about to their friends. It'd taken them weeks to find the place, but eventually they'd stumbled on it. The town, with its abandoned buildings and eerie silence, had terrified them so much they'd never gone back. Not only hadn't they returned, they rarely spoke of their experience.

"What's Bitter End got to do with Ellie?" Cal demanded.

"Nothing. What I mean is, you and I don't discuss Bitter End, and Ellie and I don't talk about our relationship because it's understood that neither of us is interested in a romance. Why's that so hard to accept?"

"Fine," Cal said with a snort of disbelief. "You believe what you want and I'll pretend not to notice the truth."

Glen was fast losing patience. "You do that, big brother." He didn't know what made Cal think he was such an expert on women. He was tempted to say so, but restrained himself. "I'll see you tonight sometime," he said, eager to set off. Ellie might act as if clearing out her childhood home was no big deal; Glen knew otherwise.

"Whenever," Cal said without apparent interest.

Glen eased Moonshine into an easy canter and headed toward the ranch house. One of these days Cal would find the right woman and that would shut him up. Glen had never been too impressed with Jennifer Healy; as far as he was concerned, Cal had made a lucky escape. Unfortunately his older brother didn't see it that way. Being ditched by his fiancée had made him cynical about women.

Switching his thoughts to Ellie, Glen smiled. He could almost see the quizzical smile she sometimes wore, could almost hear the sound of her laughter. That was what Ellie needed now—a reason to laugh. Laughter was a great emotional release, and she'd kept her feelings hidden inside for far too long.

He'd shower first, Glen decided, make himself something to eat and be on his way. Cal could sit in front of the tube if he wanted, but Glen had other plans. Much better ones.

GRADY WESTON'S throat felt parched as a dried-up creek bed. He walked into the ranch house and straight to the refrigerator. His sister, Savannah, made a tall pitcher of iced tea for him and Laredo every afternoon. Not bothering with the niceties, he reached for the glass pitcher and drank directly from that.

"Grady!" Savannah admonished him, coming into the room. Grady's old dog, Rocket, followed her, his movements slow and awkward. She carried an armful of fresh-cut old roses, their pungent scent filling the kitchen.

He finished one last swallow and set the pitcher down on the counter, then wiped his mouth with the back of his hand. "Where's Richard?" he demanded, not wanting to hear about his lack of manners.

Okay, he should've taken the time to grab a glass, but damn it all, he was tired and thirsty. He added *irritated* to the list the moment he glanced out at the drive and saw that his pickup was missing. If it turned out that his no-good brother had absconded with his truck, his irritation would quickly turn to fury.

"I...don't know where Richard is," Savannah answered, and lowered her gaze. The way she avoided meeting his eyes was a sure sign that she had her suspicions but wasn't willing to share them.

"He took the truck, didn't he?"

Savannah shrugged, then nodded.

"I figured as much," Grady growled, his anger mounting. Six years earlier Richard had stolen all the family's money and promptly disappeared. Savannah and Grady had been left to deal with the aftermath of their parents' deaths, the inheritance taxes and all the legal problems, while Richard was busy squandering every dime on God only knew what. Then, this past spring, he'd shown up, down on his luck and needing a place to live until the severance check from his last job arrived. Or so he'd told them. Savannah chose to believe Richard's story, but Grady wasn't going to trust him again. Not by a long shot.

Should've kicked him off the ranch the first day. He would have, in fact, if it hadn't been for his softhearted

sister. In the weeks since, Grady had called himself every
kind of fool. Opportunity after opportunity had presented
itself to send Richard packing, but he hadn't taken advantage of a single one.

Grady had tried to reason it out in his own mind, especially after Richard had thrown himself a welcome-home
party and stuck Grady with the bill. Deep down, Grady
recognized that he *wanted* to believe Richard had changed.
Even when every bit of evidence claimed otherwise. As the
oldest he felt a responsibility to make everything right. He
looked for ways to honor the memory of his parents. Ways
to hold on to the ranch.

Their mother had spoiled Richard; her youngest son had
been her favorite. She might be partly to blame for his self-
centered behavior, but regardless of what he'd done, she'd
have expected Grady to give him shelter. Even now, six
years after her death, Grady found himself seeking her ap-
proval.

"Where'd he go this time?" Grady asked, disgusted
more with himself than with his brother. Richard was a
master when it came to manipulating people. He was
charming and a clever conversationalist, unlike Grady who
was often loud and brusque. He wished he'd inherited some
of Richard's success with the ladies, but he was too old
and too stubborn to change now.

Savannah slowly shook her head.

"Does that mean you don't know where Richard went
or you don't want to tell me?"

"A little of both," she confessed.

Despite his anger, Grady smiled and sat down at the
table. "I probably would've given him the keys if he'd
asked," he admitted with a certain reluctance.

"I...didn't actually give him the keys, but I told him
where they were."

Savannah sat down across from him. It struck Grady how

beautiful his sister was. As little as six months ago he would never have thought of her that way. She was just Savannah, his kindhearted younger sister. A woman who rarely raised her voice, rarely disagreed. A picture of calm serenity, while he struggled to contain his explosive temper. A woman who'd always been happy with her quiet low-key life.

Then one day, out of the blue, his sister had changed. No, he corrected himself, she'd always been strong in ways that made others seem weak, but he'd failed to recognize or appreciate those qualities in her. It had been quite a lesson she'd given him. She'd begun to assert her own needs; she'd made him aware that she wanted more from life than he'd realized or been willing to acknowledge. These changes came about because of Laredo Smith, a drifter who'd stumbled into their lives. A cowboy. A god-send. Grady and Laredo were partners now. The wedding had taken place a few weeks earlier in her rose garden, with only a few close friends as guests. In time the newly-weds would be building their own home and starting a fam-ily. Grady looked forward to having children on the ranch.

Falling in love had transformed his sister into a woman of true beauty. It was as if all the goodness inside her had become outwardly visible. He wasn't the only one who'd noticed, either. A couple of months ago she'd cut her hair—formerly waist-length—and begun wearing jeans instead of those long loose dresses. All at once other men had started to take heed. Too late, however, because her heart belonged to Laredo.

"What time did he leave?" Grady asked, rubbing his face tiredly. The problems with Richard just seemed to multiply. The money he'd claimed was coming had yet to arrive, although he'd managed to reimburse Grady five hun-dred dollars.

Grady had serious doubts about any so-called severance

pay owed to Richard. He suspected the money was just the beginning of a long list of lies his brother had been feeding them.

To Grady's relief, Savannah no longer actively championed Richard's cause, and he knew she felt as troubled as he did about their younger brother. Neither was comfortable at the thought of kicking him off the ranch entirely. Besides, Richard occasionally made himself useful, running errands in town and making token efforts to help around the ranch.

"He left about three this afternoon."

"He didn't go into town, did he?"

Savannah hesitated. "I don't think so, but then, he didn't tell me where he was headed."

"I could have used an extra hand this afternoon," Grady murmured.

But they both knew Richard's answer to that. He was never cut out to be a rancher, which was the reason he'd given for fleeing with the family money—his share of the inheritance he called it, since he wanted no part of the ranch. The excuse stuck in Grady's craw every time he thought about it.

"He's been keeping himself busy," Savannah said, and held his gaze a moment longer than usual. Neither one of them was entirely sure what he did with his time. He disappeared for hours at a stretch without telling anyone where he went or who he was with. Normally Grady wouldn't care, but considering Richard's history, it was worrisome.

"I heard him talking to Ellie on the phone earlier," Savannah told him. "He invited her to Ruth's birthday party."

This didn't give Grady any cause for celebration. He'd noticed his younger brother's growing interest in Ellie Frasier. The fact that she'd recently inherited the family business hadn't escaped Richard's notice, and Grady worried that his brother's interest might be leaning more toward that feed store than to Ellie. She'd dealt with enough grief to have anyone exploit her now.

"She doesn't know, does she?" Savannah asked.

Grady shook his head. Few people in Promise were aware of Richard's crime. It was something Grady preferred not to share. No one wanted his friends and neighbors to learn that his only brother had robbed him blind. Only a handful of folks knew Richard had run off with every penny in the family coffers the day they buried their parents. Vanished for six years until he'd needed help himself.

Grady cursed under his breath and waited for Savannah to chastise him.

She didn't, and Grady soon realized why. The screen door opened and Laredo walked into the kitchen. The wrangler's gaze immediately met Savannah's and they exchanged a tender look.

They fascinated Grady. His sister and her husband were so deeply in love he doubted either one remembered he was in the room. Savannah stood and poured Laredo a glass of iced tea, which the man accepted gratefully. After downing the contents in four or five gulps, Laredo set the glass aside and hugged her close.

Grady watched his brother-in-law's eyes drift shut as he savored holding Savannah. In all his thirty-five years, Grady had never seen any two people more in love. Watching them lost in each other's embrace was almost painful, reminding him how alone he was. He realized he wasn't an easy man to love—he knew that—and he doubted any woman would put up with him for long. Yet he couldn't watch Savannah and Laredo and not wish for that kind of contentment himself.

Grady had never felt lonely before, never given much thought to marriage. *Someday* was about as close as he'd gotten to thinking about any future romance and then only if he could find a woman willing to look past his very noticeable flaws.

There hadn't been *time* to give any consideration to his marital status and romantic hopes—such as they were. It'd taken him six years of back-breaking labor to dig the ranch out of debt. If all went well with this year's herd, they'd be completely in the black once again.

"Caroline's coming over later," Savannah murmured.

Grady wasn't sure who the comment was meant for. Probably him. Nor was he sure whether she intended this as a warning or as...something else. Caroline Daniels was Savannah's best friend and the town's postmistress; he couldn't seem to get along with her, but he was afraid Savannah still had matchmaking ambitions concerning them. A completely hopeless and wrongheaded idea. Lately his sister and Caroline had spent a lot of time discussing and designing house plans, and while that didn't affect Grady one way or another, he often found himself in the company of Caroline's five-year-old daughter, Maggie. He'd been gruff and impatient with the girl not long ago, and she would barely look at him now. Grady felt bad about that.

And it irritated him no end that Maggie had taken to Richard, and being the smooth-talking charmer he was, his younger brother soon had the kid eating out of his hand.

Grady considered his squabbles with Caroline more her fault than his. He admired people who spoke their minds, but Caroline did it a little too often for his liking.

"Are you going to Ruth's birthday party?" Savannah asked.

Grady hesitated, but only for a moment. "Probably not."

His sister's eyes flared briefly and he knew that wasn't the response she'd wanted.

"Why not?"

He wasn't accustomed to explaining his decisions, but

Savannah had that look about her, and he knew it was better to deal with the subject now than postpone it.

"Do I need a reason?"

"Laredo and I are going," she said, wrapping her arm around her husband's waist. "Ruth's a sweetheart, and it means a great deal to Nell that there be a nice turnout."

"Cal's not going." Grady couldn't resist pointing this out, although he didn't feel he should have to.

"That's exactly my point," Savannah returned. "If you're not careful, you're going to end up just like Cal."

"And what's wrong with Cal?" Although he asked the question, Grady knew what she meant. Ever since Jennifer had more or less left him at the altar, Cal Patterson had little that was good to say about women. His cynical attitude got to be a bit much, even for Grady, but now wasn't the time to admit it.

"There's nothing wrong with Cal that a good woman wouldn't cure."

"Savannah would like you to ask Caroline to the party," Laredo inserted. He wasn't much of a talker, but when he did speak, he cut to the chase. No beating around the bush with Savannah's husband.

"What? You want me to *what?*" Grady pretended his hearing was impaired and stuck his finger in his ear. He thought he was pretty comical.

Savannah didn't. "Is there a problem with Caroline?" she demanded. Her eyes flashed with spirit and Grady could see it wasn't going to be easy to mollify her.

"Nope."

"You'd be fortunate if she accepted!"

"Of course I would," he agreed with more than a touch of sarcasm.

"Grady!"

Chuckling, he held up his hands in surrender. "Caroline's all right," he said. "It's just that we don't see eye to eye about a lot of things. You know that, Savannah. I like her, don't get me wrong, but I can't see the two of us dating."

"Because of Maggie?" Savannah asked.

"Not at all," Grady assured her, knowing how close Savannah and the little girl were.

"Savannah thought it'd be a good idea if the four of us went to Ruth's party together." Again it was Laredo who spelled out Savannah's intentions.

"Me and Caroline?" Grady burst out. He bent forward and slapped his hands on his knees in exaggerated hilarity. "Me and Caroline with you two?" Even more amusing. The lovebirds and him...with the postmistress. Yeah, good idea, all right. Great idea. He and Caroline could barely manage a civil word to each other. "You've got to be kidding. Tell me this is a joke."

"Apparently not." The cool voice came from the back door.

Grady's blood turned cold. Caroline Daniels and Maggie stood just inside the kitchen, and a single glance told him she'd seen his whole performance, heard every derogatory word.

Chapter Two

The boxes awaited Ellie as she unlocked her front door and stepped inside the small rented house. Stacked against the far living-room wall, they represented what felt like an insurmountable task. She paused, her eyes drawn to the piled-up cartons. If she was smart, she'd move them out of sight and deal with the emotional nightmare of sorting through her father's things when she was better able to handle it.

But she wouldn't put this off. Again she was her father's daughter, and he'd taught her never to procrastinate. The thought of those boxes would hound her until she'd gone through every last one of them.

A number of delaying tactics occurred to her. There were letters to write, phone calls to make, people to thank; nevertheless, she recognized them for the excuses they were. The remains of her father's life would still be there, demanding her attention. Occupying her mind.

It would be easy to focus her anger on her mother, but Ellie was mature enough to recognize and accept that Pam Frasier had been pampered all her life. She'd been indulged and shielded from all unpleasantness from the time she was a child. First by her family and then by her husband. John Frasier had treated his wife like a delicate Southern blossom and protected her like the gentle knight he was.

His lengthy illness had taken a toll on Ellie's mother. To

her credit Pam had done the best she could, sitting by his side for long periods at the hospital. But unfortunately she had required almost as much care and attention as her husband; she had trouble dealing with any form of illness and was horrified by the thought of death. And so, comforting John had mostly fallen to Ellie.

Dealing with John's effects, coping with the memories, was just one more obligation her mother couldn't manage. Heaving a sigh, Ellie rolled up her sleeves and tackled the first box.

Clothes. Work clothes the movers had packed. Ellie lovingly ran her hand over his favorite sweater, the elbows patched with leather. Pam had wanted him to throw it out— too old and shabby, she'd said. It astonished Ellie that her parents had ever married, as different as they were. They'd met while her father was in the service, and although no one had said as much, Ellie was convinced her mother had fallen in love with the uniform. Their courtship was far too short, and all too soon they were married and John was out of the army. He'd returned to Promise with his bride and joined his father at the family feed store. Ellie had been born two years later, after a difficult pregnancy. John had assured his wife he was perfectly content with one child and there was no need for more. Even as a young girl Ellie had realized her father intended to groom her to take over the store. Not once had she thought of doing anything else. She'd majored in business at the University of Texas at Austin, and although she'd dated several young men, she'd never allowed any relationship to grow serious. She couldn't, not when it was understood she'd be returning to Promise and the feed store. After graduation, she'd found a small house to rent a few blocks from her parents and started working with her dad.

Ellie kept the sweater, but rather than unpack the rest of the clothes, she set the box aside, along with the next two,

all of which contained items from his closet. The local char-
ities were always in need of good clothes, and it would be
an easy matter to drop them off.

When she opened the fourth box, Ellie paused. The old
family Bible rested on top of a photo album. Carefully,
using both hands, she lifted the fragile book from its card-
board shelter. The Bible had been in her father's family for
a hundred-plus years, handed down from one generation to
the next. Ellie had known about it; she'd read the names
listed in the front for a high-school report years before, but
hadn't opened it since. In fact, she wasn't sure where her
mother had stored it.

Curious, she sat down on the sofa and set the book on
the coffee table. Leaning forward, she opened it. Once
again she read the names listed, reacquainting herself with
each one, recalling what her father had told her about her
ancestors.

Her great-great grandparents, Jeremiah and Esther Frasier—good Biblical names, Ellie mused—together with their
three sons, whose births were also noted, had placed all
their worldly possessions in a covered wagon. Then with
courage and faith they'd ventured west, risking all for the
promise of land in Texas.

Ellie ran her index finger down the names of the three
children, pausing over the youngest, Edward Abraham. His
birthday was recorded and then the date of his death only
five years later. No reason was listed, only a tear-smudged
Bible reference. *Matthew 28:46.* Not recognizing it, Ellie
flipped the pages until she located the verse. *"My God, my
God, why have you forsaken me."*

The agony of Esther's loss seemed to vibrate from the
page. With her own heart still fragile from the pain of her
father's death, Ellie was keenly aware of this young
mother's anguish over the loss of her son. Unable to read
more, she closed the Bible and put it aside.

As she did, a single piece of cloth slipped from between the pages and drifted onto the coffee table. Ellie reached for it and frowned. The muslin square had yellowed with age; each side was no bigger than six inches. In the middle of the block was an embroidered bug that resembled a giant grasshopper. The detail was exquisite, each infinitesimally small stitch perfectly positioned. Nevertheless, it was an odd thing to place inside a Bible. What could possibly have been important enough about an embroidered grasshopper to save it all these years, tucked between the pages of a family Bible? But these were questions for another time, another day.

Her stomach growled and, glancing at her watch, Ellie realized it'd been almost six hours since she'd last eaten. She carried the Bible into her bedroom and placed it on her dresser top, then rummaged around her kitchen until she found the ingredients for a tuna salad.

An hour later a half-eaten salad and an empty milk glass on the carpet beside her, Ellie happened upon the box of John Wayne videos. Her father had loved the Duke. In the worst days of his illness, it was the one thing that was sure to calm him. These movies were as much a part of his heritage as the family Bible. She placed them in the cabinet below her television and on impulse inserted one into the VCR.

McLintock! with Maureen O'Hara was one of Ellie's favorites. Soon she found herself involved in the movie, the boxes forgotten. She didn't have to unpack *every* box that night, she decided.

With the lights dimmed she sat cross-legged on the sofa, watching the television screen. This particular John Wayne classic had been a favorite of her father's as well. Only a few months earlier, he'd suggested that when Ellie decided to look for a husband, she wouldn't go wrong if she found a man like the kind John Wayne usually portrayed.

Where the tears came from, Ellie didn't know. One moment she was laughing at the very place she laughed every time she saw the movie, and the next her cheeks were wet with tears.

Chastising herself for being too sentimental, she dried her eyes with a napkin. A minute later, the tears started again. Soon they flowed with such vigor she required a box of tissues.

It didn't take Ellie long to realize that the movie had triggered the release she'd needed all these weeks. Stopping the flow of tears was impossible, so she gave up trying, sobbing openly now. With a tissue pressed to each eye, she sniffed, then paused, holding her breath, thinking she'd heard a noise unrelated to the movie.

The sound was repeated and Ellie groaned.

The doorbell.

She yearned to ignore it, but anyone who knew her would recognize her car parked out front.

With a reluctant sigh, she walked slowly toward the door. She glanced through the peephole, but whoever was there had moved out of her range of vision.

"Who's there?" she demanded.

"The big bad wolf."

Glen.

"Damn," she muttered under her breath, frantically rubbing at the tears on her face. "Go away," she called out. "I'm not decent." Which wasn't far from the truth. He was her friend and a good one but she didn't want him or anyone else to see her like this.

"Come on, Ellie, open up."

"Not by the hair of your chinny, chin, chin," she called back.

"Then I'll huff and I'll puff and I'll blow your house down."

She hesitated, unsure what to do.

"Ellie, for heaven's sake, grab a towel or whatever and let me in."

He twisted the knob and she realized he was going to enter with or without her permission. This was what she got for not keeping her front door locked, but it was a habit she'd never developed. No need to in a town like Promise.

"Come on in," she said, finally opening the door.

"You're dressed," he said with some surprise. "I thought you said—" Apparently he noticed her tear-blotched face, because he stopped short.

She squared her shoulders, not knowing what he'd do or say. They'd laughed together, disagreed, teased and joked, but she'd never allowed Glen or anyone else to see her cry.

His hand rested gently on her shoulder. "I thought as much," he whispered.

It would have been better if he'd made a joke of it, Ellie mused. She might have been able to laugh off her embarrassment if he had.

"It's the movie," she said, pointing to the television set behind her. "I...started watching it and..." To her utter humiliation, the tears came back in force.

"Ellie?"

She turned her back to him. "I'm not fit company just now," she managed.

"Do you want me to leave?" he asked from behind.

Did she? Ellie didn't know. Wrapping her arms around her middle, she couldn't remember a time she'd felt more alone. Her beloved father was gone and her mother had all but abandoned her. It wasn't supposed to happen like this. Her father had been everything to her.

"Ellie?" Glen questioned again.

"You'd better go."

A long moment passed. Anyone else would have left by now, but Glen hesitated, as though he couldn't make him-

self do it. That was when Ellie knew she wanted him to
stay.

"Would...would you mind sticking around for a
while?" she choked out.

"Of course." With his arm loosely about her shoulders,
he steered her back to the sofa. "Sit here and I'll get you
something to drink."

She nodded, grateful once again that Glen Patterson was
her friend. A good stiff drink was exactly what she needed.
Something strong enough to dull the pain.

Within a couple of minutes Glen returned with a tall
glass. Ice clinked against the sides when he handed it to
her.

She appreciated his tact and understanding and accepted
the glass. Tentatively tasting the drink, she tried to remember what she had stored in the liquor cabinet above the
refrigerator. Vodka? Gin?

Almost immediately she started to cough and choke.

Glen slapped her hard on the back.

She needed a moment to catch her breath. When she did
she glared at him with narrowed eyes. "You brought me
ice water?" she cried. The man had no sense of what she
was suffering. None whatsoever, or he'd realize that a time
like this required liquor.

"What's wrong with water?" he asked with a look of
such genuine innocence that Ellie knew it would do no
good to explain.

She dismissed his question with a wave of her hand and
gestured for him to sit down.

Glen claimed the empty space next to her on the sofa.
"Do you want to talk about it?" he asked.

"No," she said, and for emphasis shook her head. "Just
watch the movie."

"All right." He leaned back and stretched his arms along

the back of the couch. With one foot resting on the other knee, he seemed perfectly at ease.

Ellie did her best to focus on the movie, but it was pointless. So was any attempt to hold back the tears that pooled in her eyes, then leaked from the corners, making wet tracks down the sides of her face. At first she tried to blink them away. That didn't help. Neither did holding her breath or staring up at the ceiling. She drank the glass of water and, when she could disguise the need no longer, made a frantic grab for the box of tissue.

"I thought as much," Glen said for the second time. He placed his arm around her shoulders and pulled her against him. "It isn't the movie, is it?"

"What makes you ask that?" she sobbed.

"Because I know you."

Men always assumed they knew a woman when they didn't have a clue. And Glen Patterson was as clueless as any man she'd ever known, friend or not.

"As I said earlier, I'm not very good company at the moment." She blotted her eyes with a fresh tissue. In an effort to distract her thoughts, she showed him the old Bible with the names of family who'd lived and died over a hundred years ago. When she talked about Edward Abraham's death, the tears began again.

"Hey, if I'd been looking for scintillating company, I would've stayed home with Cal," Glen said, then laughed at his little joke.

They both knew Cal was about as much fun as a rampaging bull these days.

"Come on," he urged with real tenderness. "Let it all out."

She swallowed a sob. It would have been better, she thought now, if he hadn't stayed, after all. But it felt good to lean on someone. So good. Ellie feared that once she lowered her guard and gave way to her emotions, it would be like a river overflowing its banks. All semblance of control would vanish. As close a friend as Glen was, she preferred to shed her tears alone.

"Relax," he instructed, sounding like the older brother she'd never had. He squeezed her shoulder and rested his chin against her hair. "It's okay to cry. You have the right."

"I couldn't make myself believe it," she sobbed into his chest. The doctors had explained soon after he was diagnosed that his condition was terminal. No hope.

"Believe what?" Glen asked softly.

"That he was dying. I should have been prepared for it, but I wasn't."

"He was your father, Ellie. How could you prepare to lose your father? How could anyone?"

"I—I don't know." Her whole body shook; she couldn't control the tremors.

"Quit being so hard on yourself, okay?"

"I wanted to celebrate his life," she added. "Not...not act like this." She felt as though she were walking around with a giant hole inside her. Grief overwhelmed her. She missed him in a thousand different ways. Every minute, every hour, she found reasons to think of him. Everything she said and did reminded her of how close they'd always been. She couldn't walk into the store without confronting evidence of him—his work, his personality, his plans for the future. If that wasn't bad enough, every time she looked in the mirror it was his deep blue eyes that stared back.

"You *are* celebrating his life," Glen murmured, and his lips brushed the top of her head.

"I am?" Easing herself from his embrace, she raised her face to look up at him.

"You were the apple of your father's eye," Glen reminded her. "He couldn't keep the buttons of his shirt fastened, he was so proud of you."

While Ellie knew that was true, it felt good to hear Glen say it. "He was a wonderful father." She bit her lower lip to keep it from trembling.

"The best." Glen gazed down at her and with his thumb caught a tear as it rolled from her bottom lashes and onto her cheek.

He paused with his finger halfway across her face and when her vision cleared, Ellie noted Glen's look of surprise. Their eyes met, widened. They couldn't seem to stop gazing at each other's faces. Ellie suddenly felt herself frowning, but before she had a chance to analyze what was happening, she realized something else.

Glen was going to kiss her.

She could have moved, avoided his kiss and the embarrassment that was sure to follow, but curiosity got the better of her. As his mouth slowly lowered toward hers, her eyes drifted shut. She half expected him to draw back at the last second, but he didn't—and she was glad.

His lips were moist and warm as they settled gently on hers. The gentleness lasted only a moment, and then he thrust his fingers into her short hair and increased the pressure of his mouth. Ellie felt the heat in him, the unaccustomed desire. And she felt his tension. She understood it, because she was feeling the same thing. A sense of discomfort, even guilt. This was Glen, her friend. And they were kissing like lovers, like a couple well beyond the range of friendship.

Ellie slipped her hands up his chest and anchored her fingers at his shoulders. The kiss took on another dimension. The hunger that had been held in check was replaced by heady excitement. Ellie opened to Glen without restraint, reserving nothing. He deepened the kiss until they both trembled. When he abruptly broke it off, his breathing was heavy and labored. So was hers.

Slowly Ellie opened her eyes. Glen was staring at her, his forehead creased in a deep frown.

"What was that?" she asked, her voice barely above a whisper.

"A kiss," he said, sounding almost angry.

"I know that. What I'm asking is...why?"

"Why?" he repeated, sounding as uncertain as she was. "Because...because you were crying."

"So?"

"It was shock therapy," he said, easing himself away from her, gently at first and then as if he couldn't move fast enough. He scooted unceremoniously to the side of the sofa.

Not knowing what to think, much less say, she blinked.

"It worked," he said, as if this entire incident had been carefully planned. "You're not crying, are you?"

Ellie raised her fingertips to her face. He was right.

"I had to do *something*," he said, sounding more like himself now—confident, amused, down-to-earth.

"Something," she repeated, trying not to press her fingers against her slightly swollen lips.

"Anything," he added. "I was getting desperate. You feel better, don't you?"

She had to consider that for a moment. But it was true.

"Hey, I didn't mean..." He hesitated as if not sure how to continue.

Ellie wasn't sure she wanted him to. "Me neither," she told him quickly, far more comfortable dropping the matter than exploring it further. Glen was a damn good friend and she didn't want one stupid kiss to ruin this friendship.

He relaxed visibly. "Good."

She smiled and nodded. "I gotta admit, though," she said, eagerly falling back on the comfortable banter they'd always enjoyed. "You're one fine kisser."

"Damn fine," he agreed, and puffed out his chest in a

parody of male pride. "You aren't the first one to tell me that."

Ellie rolled her eyes toward the ceiling.

"You aren't so bad yourself."

"Don't I know it." Standing, she hooked her thumbs in the belt loops of her jeans and rocked on her heels. "Plenty of other guys have told me I'm hot stuff."

"I can see why."

They laughed then, both of them, but Ellie noticed that their laughter had a decidedly shaky sound to it.

"SHAKY" PRETTY WELL described how Glen felt. An hour later he pulled into the long driveway that led from the highway to the Lonesome Coyote Ranch. He trembled every time he thought about kissing Ellie.

Fool that he was, he'd given in to a crazy impulse and damn near made the biggest mistake of his life.

Glen blamed Cal for this. His brother was the one who'd planted the idea, claiming Glen's relationship with Ellie was far more than friendship. Cal had just said it a few too many times and hell—Glen shook his head—one minute he was looking down at Ellie and the next thing he knew they were kissing. What scared the living daylights out of him was how incredibly good the kiss had been. It wasn't *supposed* to be that good, but it had shot straight off the Richter scale.

Oh, yeah, Ellie had shaken him up plenty.

Thank goodness he'd been able to make light of the incident, brush it off. Ellie had seemed just as eager to put it behind them. For the first time in years he'd been uncomfortable with his best friend. With Ellie. All because of an impulsive kiss, something that never should've happened.

He parked the truck and sat in the stillness of the night to gather his wits about him. He recalled how the kiss had ended and she'd looked up at him, her striking blue eyes wide with shock. Damn if it hadn't taken every ounce of willpower he possessed not to kiss her again.

Thank God he hadn't. Gratitude welled up inside him. Had they continued much longer they would've ruined everything. Knowing he was being less than subtle about it, he'd gotten the hell out of that house. Again Ellie had obviously felt relieved to be rid of him. With any luck they'd both forget the entire incident. For his part he never intended to mention it again, and he sincerely hoped Ellie didn't, either.

Once he felt sufficiently calm, he climbed out of the truck and walked into the house. Cal sat in the kitchen with ledgers spread out across the table. He glanced up when Glen entered the room and did a double take.

"You okay?"

"Why shouldn't I be?" Glen demanded sharply.

"No need to bite my head off," his brother snapped back. "What happened? You have a spat with Ellie?"

"No."

"I see," Cal returned, not bothering to suppress a smile.

"I'm going to bed," Glen announced.

"Good idea," Cal called after him. "Sleep might improve your disposition."

Glen stomped up the stairs and was breathless by the time he entered his bedroom. He closed the door and sagged onto the edge of the mattress. With his elbows resting on his knees, he inhaled deeply several times. No wonder he was shaking. He'd had a narrow escape.

THE NIGHT WAS ALIVE with sound. The intoxicating aroma of old roses filled the air. Katydids chirped and the porch swing creaked as Savannah and Laredo swayed back and forth, back and forth. The stars were generous with their glittering bounty that night. It all said *romance*, the romance of song and story, and it suited Savannah's mood perfectly.

She leaned her head against Laredo's shoulder and his arm held her close. Even now, resting in her husband's strong embrace, she found it difficult to believe this wonderful man loved her.

"What's on your mind?" he whispered.

Savannah's lips eased into a ready smile. "I was just thinking how fortunate I am that you love me."

Laredo went still, and she knew his thoughts; he didn't need to voice them. It was that way sometimes when people were deeply in love. Their marriage was like a miracle, an unexpected gift—and it had come when they were least prepared for it. Because of that, they'd come close to losing it all.

"I loved you when I left you," Laredo said, his voice hoarse with the intensity of his feelings. "I worry sometimes that you don't know how difficult it was to walk away from you."

"I did know, and that's what made it so hard," she confided. She would never fully comprehend it, but Laredo had believed that she deserved someone who could give her more than he could. It was one of life's cruel ironies—without him, money, land and possessions meant very little. But with his love she was rich beyond measure. It was the most precious thing she'd ever had.

The kitchen door creaked open and Savannah's older brother stepped onto the porch. She wasn't too pleased with Grady's poor timing, but decided to overlook it. Not for the first time, either. Look what he'd done just the other day, when he'd made those comments about Caroline at the worst possible moment.

Grady walked to the porch steps and stared into the night sky. "I decided to attend the birthday bash for Ruth," he said without glancing in their direction.

Savannah heard the reluctance in his voice and realized the decision hadn't been an easy one.

"With Caroline?" she asked, trying not to sound eager.

He hesitated before answering. "I thought about asking her, then decided against it."

Savannah knew that if he let himself Grady would enjoy Caroline's company. Unfortunately he bungled all her efforts at playing matchmaker. What she'd hoped was that he'd become comfortable enough with Caroline at the birthday party to invite her to the Cattlemen's Association dance later in the month. The dance marked the beginning of summer and was the most anticipated event of the year.

"Why *don't* you ask Caroline?" She was losing patience with him.

"Because I didn't think she'd want to after the way... Hell, you should know the answer to that. I made a fool of myself."

"Caroline was more amused than angry," Savannah assured her brother.

"Yeah, well, that's not how I saw it. I thought I'd invite someone else."

"Like who?"

"I don't know..."

"How about the new doctor?" Savannah suggested. Dr. Jane Dickinson had replaced Doc Cummings at the Health Clinic when he retired. She'd read in the local newspaper that Dr. Dickinson had agreed to stay on for three years as a means of repaying her medical-school loans. If Grady wasn't going to ask Caroline, then this new doctor was a good choice.

"No, thanks."

"What's wrong with *her?*"

"Nothing...everything." Grady didn't elaborate.

The problem with her brother, Savannah realized, was a complete lack of confidence in himself when it came to women. Grady failed to recognize his own masculine appeal. His *considerable* appeal. She suspected that Richard's presence made it worse. Richard was handsome and sociable, a smooth talker who had no difficulty attracting female companionship. Grady, on the other hand, was awkward around women and constantly seemed to say the wrong thing.

Savannah edged closer to her husband. "Um, Grady, I don't think it's a good idea to wait until the last minute."

"You don't?"

Both Savannah and Laredo shook their heads.

Grady rubbed the back of his neck. "The hell with it," he muttered. "Nell didn't say anything about bringing a date. If Cal shows up you can bet he'll be without a woman. Nothing says I need one, either."

Savannah resisted the urge to box his ears. "Do you intend to live the rest of your life alone, Grady?"

Her brother didn't answer her for a moment. "I don't know anymore. It just seems to be the way things are headed." With that, he went back inside.

"I almost feel sorry for him," Laredo said.

"It's his own fault." Savannah didn't mean to sound unkind, but her brother was too stubborn for his own good. "If he'd open his eyes, he'd realize Caroline's perfect for him."

"You can't push him into a relationship with your friend, love."

Savannah realized that. "But…"

"It'll happen for Grady when the time is right."

"How can you be so sure?"

"It did with us."

Sighing, Savannah dropped her head against his shoulder once again. This was her favorite time of day, sitting in the moonlight with Laredo, feeling his love enclose her.

They kissed then, and the sweetness of it was enough to

bring tears to Savannah's eyes. She savored the contentment of being in his arms, wishing everyone could experience this kind of love. Grady and the embittered Cal Patterson and Caroline and...

"Ellie Frasier needs someone, too," she said wistfully.

"Are you the resident matchmaker now?" Laredo teased.

"Yes—even if it *is* self-appointed." She nudged him with her elbow. "Now—a man for Ellie."

"Not Richard."

"Not Richard," Savannah agreed. "Glen Patterson."

Laredo laughed lightly. "You're way off base with that one, Savannah. I can't see it. They make much better friends than they ever would lovers."

The evening was much too fine to argue. She didn't need Laredo to agree with her to know she was right.

Chapter Three

Nell Bishop flipped the braid off her shoulder and surveyed the yard. Everything was ready for Ruth's surprise party. The Moorhouse sisters, both retired schoolteachers, were keeping her mother-in-law occupied in town. Knowing Edwina and Lily, they'd take their assignment seriously. The last Nell heard, they'd planned a visit to the library, followed by a little birthday celebration at Dovie Boyd's antique shop. Dovie had recently added the Victorian Tea Room, and each afternoon at three, she served tea and scones. Sometimes she added cucumber sandwiches and a small glass—or two—of the Moorhouse sisters' special cordial, which she made from a recipe handed down by their maternal grandfather.

Nell gathered that the sandwiches tended to be dry but the cordial was well worth the price of admission. The Moorhouse sisters would bring her back at the start of the festivities. All three would probably be a little tipsy and in a fine party mood.

It was time the Bishop family did a bit of celebrating. Jake wouldn't have wanted them to spend the rest of their lives grieving. Things had been difficult for Nell since her husband's death, but with Ruth's help she'd managed to hold on to the ranch.

"Mom, where do you want me to put the potato chips?"

Jeremy called from the back porch steps. Her eleven-year-old son stood with a huge bowl in his hands, awaiting her instructions.

"Set it on the first picnic table," she answered, pointing at the line of five covered tables that stretched across the freshly groomed yard. She'd spent half the day spiffing up the flower beds and mowing the grass and the other half cooking. Fried chicken, her special recipe for chili, a smorgasbord of salads, plus a huge homemade birthday cake.

Jeremy carried the bowl to the table, then promptly helped himself to a handful. Nell bit her tongue to keep from admonishing him not to spoil his dinner. This was a celebration and she wasn't going to ruin it by scolding her children. Both Jeremy and nine-year-old Emma had been helpful and cooperative, as excited about the party as she was herself.

Jeremy's hand stopped midway to his mouth and he cast a guilty look at his mother.

"All I ask is that you save some for the guests."

He nodded, smiling hugely. "We got plenty."

How like Jake her son was. She couldn't look at him and not be reminded of the only man she'd ever loved. They'd grown up together, she and Jake, and Nell knew from the time she'd first started thinking about boys that one day she'd marry Jake Bishop. It had taken him several years to reach the same conclusion, but men were often slower when it came to figuring out these things.

Both Nell and Jake were tall and big-boned. Nell was nearly six feet by the time she stopped growing. She had the kind of looks that were usually described as handsome, not pretty. And certainly not cute. The only man she'd ever known who hadn't been intimidated by her size—or treated her like one of the boys—had been Jake, and that was because he was six feet four inches himself.

Jake had taught her the wonders of being feminine.

They'd had almost ten years together, and she'd treasured every one of them. Some folks expected her to remarry, but she'd yet to meet the man who could match the husband she'd lost. Nell wasn't willing to accept second best, not after loving Jake.

For the first year after Jake's death in a tractor accident she'd felt cheated and angry. It had taken her another year to accept his death and to reshape her life now that her husband was gone. With his mother's love and support she'd been able to keep the ranch, raise her kids, plan for the future.

She was a good cook, an able manager and, thanks to Jake, knew a great deal about ranching. More than she'd ever wanted to learn, in fact. The time had come to put all that knowledge to good use.

The party was to serve a dual purpose. To celebrate Ruth's birthday of course. And also to announce that she was opening her doors and turning Twin Canyon into a dude ranch. By the end of next year she hoped to be giving a group of greenhorns a taste of the real Texas.

Her research had shown that the cowboy era was alive and well in the minds of adventurous Americans. The travel agents she'd spoken with had assured her they could fill the bunkhouse with tourists eager to spend their vacation dollars learning about life in the Old West.

And Nell was just the one to teach them. She'd feed them her chili, get them on the back of a horse and demonstrate how to herd a few head of cattle. Take them on a trail drive—like in the movie *City Slickers*. And after all that, she'd gladly accept their credit cards.

"Mom!" Emma called, her freckled face smeared with frosting from the birthday cake. "Should I put the candles in now?"

"Not yet."

"Hey!" Jeremy hollered. "*I* was supposed to lick the

beaters!'' He grabbed a fresh supply of potato chips, apparently to compensate for the frosting he'd missed.

"Wash your face,'' Nell instructed her daughter. "I need your help out here.''

"Yeah,'' Jeremy said with an air of superiority. "Help Mom.''

"I am,'' Emma insisted. "I tasted the frosting to make sure it was good.''

Despite herself, Nell laughed. "Come on, you two. The party's going to start soon and I want all the food on the tables, ready for the buffet.'' She headed for the house to collect paper plates and napkins.

"Will Grandma be surprised?'' Emma asked.

Nell knew how hard it had been for her daughter to keep the birthday party a secret. "Very,'' she promised. "And Grandma's going to have a wonderful time. We all are.''

She was sure of it.

THE BIRTHDAY PARTY was already in full swing when Ellie and Richard arrived. People clustered about the yard, talking in small groups. There was an air of joy and festivity that Ellie found infectious. Party sounds—laughter, animated conversation and music—were everywhere. Ellie began to hope she might actually enjoy herself the way she used to.

She glanced around and realized she was looking for Glen. Although she'd agreed to attend the party with Richard Weston, she wished now that she'd turned him down.

She hadn't seen Glen in three days. Not since he'd kissed her. Hadn't heard from him, either. While it wasn't unusual for them to go a week or longer without talking to each other, for some reason this three-day stretch felt more like three months.

She had no intention of mentioning the kiss, but that didn't mean she hadn't been thinking about it. As a matter of fact, she'd thought of little else, and she wondered if the incident weighed as heavy on Glen's mind as it did hers.

Probably not.

"I should have brought my guitar," Richard said, pressing his hand against her back as he steered her into the yard.

Richard had a fairly good singing voice and he'd entertained a crowd at his welcome-home party a few months earlier. He seemed quite impressed with his musical talent—excessively so, in Ellie's opinion. Although his voice was pleasant, it would assure him a position in the church choir but nowhere else.

"Did I tell you how beautiful you look this evening?" he asked.

"Twice," she murmured. One thing about Richard, he was a charmer. His remarks were nice to hear, but she didn't take them seriously.

"I'm pleased to see you're keeping track of how often I say it," he muttered with a tinge of sarcasm.

Ellie gave him a sharp look. She was well aware of the kind of man Richard Weston was. She'd seen him in action and had to admire his skill. He issued his compliments with just enough wonder in his voice to sound sincere. Some women might believe him, but she wouldn't allow herself to be deluded. She also suspected that Richard didn't like her perceptiveness.

Ellie was delighted to see that Nell had gotten the big turnout she'd wanted. No one ever came right out and said it, but the town was proud of Nell Bishop. They were attending this party as much for her as for Ruth. Folks wanted Nell to know they respected the way she'd managed to keep the ranch in operation. The way she'd stood against popular opinion and refused to sell. At the first sign of financial difficulty, a lot of well-meaning friends had suggested she get rid of the ranch. Ellie wasn't sure she would have advised otherwise, but Nell had insisted on keeping the small spread. It had been her husband's heritage; now it was her children's. More than that, Ellie realized, the ranch was part of Jake, and Nell had deeply loved her husband.

"Help yourself to a plate," Richard urged as they neared the picnic tables. Ellie surveyed the wide assortment of hot dishes and salads. From the look of it, Nell had cooked everything herself.

A card table was stacked with brightly wrapped birthday presents, and Ellie added hers to the pile. Busy seeing to some other guests, Nell waved a hand in greeting and Ellie waved back. Ruth sat in the seat of honor, a rocking chair, with her friends circled around her. The older woman, who was normally quiet and reserved, appeared to relish being the center of attention. Jeremy and Emma raced about the yard with several other children in hot pursuit.

"You ready to eat?" Richard asked, sounding as if it'd been at least a year since he'd last sat down to a decent meal.

"Sure." Ellie reached for a paper plate and suddenly, out of the corner of her eye, caught sight of Glen. She turned slightly and noticed that he sat under the shade of an oak tree chatting with Grady Weston. He seemed to see her at the same time, and their eyes locked and held for an embarrassingly long moment. Any other time she would've waved and gestured for him to save her a place. But not now. Instead, she pretended she hadn't seen him and proceeded down the buffet line.

Apparently Richard was aware of the moment and staked his claim by sliding his arm about her waist and nuzzling her neck. Ellie didn't dare look in Glen's direction for fear of what he'd think.

"Richard," she murmured under her breath. "Stop it."

"Stop what?" he asked. "I can't help if it I find you irresistible."

"Yeah, right." What he found her, Ellie surmised, was a trophy. The victor's spoils, to wave beneath Glen's nose. Although close in age, Richard and Glen had never been friendly, and while they weren't openly hostile to each other, there was no love lost, either.

Ellie filled her plate and tried to ignore Richard as he added a spoonful of this and that, insisting she sample every dish. Considering all the attention he paid her, anyone might have assumed they were a longtime couple. All this solicitude embarrassed her.

"Would you kindly stop?" she said, and despite her displeasure, she laughed at the woebegone look he wore.

"I can't help myself," he said. "You're the most beautiful woman here." Ellie just shook her head.

They found an empty space on the grass, shaded by the house. The scent of freshly mowed lawn and a row of blooming roses mingled with the sights and sounds of the party.

Far more aware of Glen than she wanted to be, Ellie talked nervously, telling Richard about her week. He didn't pay much attention until she mentioned the old family Bible she'd found among her father's things.

"How old did you say it was?"

"More than a hundred years," Ellie answered. Although there were a number of dates entered in the Bible, she wasn't sure when it had first been purchased.

"Your ancestors were part of the original group that settled in Bitter End?"

"From what I understand they were."

"Have you ever been there?" Richard surprised her by asking next.

The question was ridiculous. No one had, no one she knew, anyway. Bitter End was a mysterious almost mythical town people whispered about. Its location remained a secret, and despite her childhood curiosity, her father had told her very little. But as far as she could figure, there simply wasn't that much to tell. The town had been settled shortly after the Civil War and for unknown reasons was later abandoned. A scattering of the original settlers—Ellie's ancestors among them—then founded Promise.

Richard's eyes darted around as if to gauge whether anyone was listening in on their conversation. "I've been to Bitter End," he whispered dramatically. "Not that long ago, either."

"Get out of here!" It was all a joke and she wasn't going to fall for it. If she did, he'd laugh at her for believing him, and she didn't want to be the brunt of his teasing remarks.

His eyes narrowed and he bent toward her. "I'm serious, Ellie."

If Bitter End was anywhere in the vicinity, people would be flocking to it—ghost towns were fascinating, this one particularly so because of the mystery surrounding the original settlers' departure.

"Have you noticed that people don't talk about it much?" he asked, lowering his voice again. He made it sound as though the residents of Promise had conspired to keep the town a secret—to which *he* held the key.

Ellie frowned, unwilling to play his nonsensical game.

"It isn't called a ghost town for nothing." Richard shivered as if a sudden chill had raced up his spine.

"Richard," she snapped, "if this is a joke, I'm not amused."

His expression was earnest as he shook his head. "I swear to you on my parents' grave I'm serious."

"You've seen Bitter End yourself?" Even now she wasn't sure she should believe him.

"Yes," he insisted. "So have others."

"Who?" She didn't know anyone who'd been to the ghost town, and she'd spent her entire life in Promise.

"Glen Patterson for one."

Now she *knew* he was joking. Glen was her best friend, and he would certainly have mentioned this if it was true.

Richard must have read the doubt in her eyes because he added, "He found it, along with my brother and Cal, when he was a kid. If you don't believe me, ask him yourself."

Ellie intended on doing exactly that.

"When were you last there?" she asked, still feeling suspicious.

"Recently."

"How recently?"

"This week."

Ellie's curiosity went into overdrive. "You'd better not be razzing me, Richard."

"I swear it's the truth."

"Will you take me there?"

He hesitated.

"Richard, you can't tell me about Bitter End and then refuse to show it to me! What's it like? Where is it? Are any of the old buildings still standing? And how in heaven's name did you find it?"

Chuckling, he held up his hand to stop her. "Whoa! One question at a time."

"All right," she said, her heart pounding with excitement. She wanted to see this place. Her father's great-grandparents had settled there. It was in Bitter End that they'd buried their five-year-old son, the child whose name was in the old Bible.

"How'd you ever find it?" she asked again.

"It wasn't easy," he said, licking his fingertips and seeming to savor her attention as much as he did Nell's fried chicken. "I knew it was real because I'd heard…the others talk about it years ago, but they refused to tell me where it was. So I started looking on my own a few weeks ago—and I found it."

"Why wouldn't they tell you?"

"For the same reason I'm not telling you."

"Oh, no, you don't!" She wasn't going to let him pull that on her.

"Ellie," he murmured, his gaze pinning hers, "it's haunted."

"I ain't afraid of no ghosts," she teased, quoting the popular movie *Ghostbusters*.

Always quick with a laugh or a smile, Richard revealed neither. "I'm not joking."

"I'm not, either. I want you to take me there."

He shook his head, obviously regretting that he'd ever brought up the subject. "That's not a good idea."

"Then I'll have Glen take me."

Richard's face hardened. "It's dangerous there, Ellie. Anything can happen. I wouldn't feel right about taking you to someplace like Bitter End."

"I don't care. I want to see it. Just once," she pleaded.

Again he hesitated.

"Please?" she asked softly.

Richard sighed, and Ellie's gaze drifted to Glen, partly because she was curious about what he was doing, but also as a subtle message. If Richard wouldn't take her, odds were she could convince Glen to.

"All right, all right," he muttered irritably.

"When?"

"Soon."

"Tomorrow?"

Richard looked decidedly uncomfortable. "I...I don't know."

"We'll make a day of it," she coaxed, eager to explore the old town. Besides, Richard might change his mind if she didn't act quickly.

"You can't tell *anyone*."

"Why not?"

"Ellie, you don't seem to understand how serious this is. It was a mistake to mention it in the first place."

"Okay," she said, knowing that if she didn't agree he'd never take her there. "I won't tell anyone else."

"I want your word of honor," Richard insisted. "I'm not kidding, Ellie. The place is dangerous, and I don't want some fool kid to break his neck because you let word out. The minute kids around here know about it, you can bet someone's going to get hurt. I don't want that on my conscience."

Ellie didn't want it on hers, either. "You have my word, Richard."

He nodded, apparently accepting her promise. "I'll take you tomorrow afternoon, then. Be ready by two."

DESPITE HIS BEST intentions, Glen couldn't keep his eyes off Ellie and Richard. They sat huddled together, their heads close, deep in conversation. He would've sworn Ellie was too smart to be taken in by a charlatan like Richard Weston. Okay, so maybe Richard was on the level—Glen didn't really know, for Grady was as reluctant to talk about his brother as he was about everything else.

"Looks like Ellie and Richard might have more in common than I realized," Glen muttered. He noted the concerned expression on Grady's face.

"I'd say she's pretty vulnerable right now," Grady commented. He seemed to be asking Glen to keep an eye on Ellie. "Someone needs to watch out for her."

Glen's own concerns mounted. He didn't like the way those two were gazing at each other—as though nobody else was around. In fact, it bothered him. *Really* bothered him.

"How good a friend are you?" Grady asked.

"Good." Good enough for him to kiss her, Glen mused. Not just any kiss, either, but one that had damn near knocked his socks off. He'd thought of little else for three days and three sleepless nights. Every time he closed his eyes she was there in his mind, and damn it all, he found himself wanting to kiss her again.

He worried that he'd ruined their friendship, and from her reaction when she arrived at the party, that looked all too likely. As for the way things were developing between her and Richard—well, he didn't trust Grady's younger brother, not one bit. The guy was too glib, too smooth. And that was only the half of it.

Glen had heard from Cal how Grady got stuck with the bill for Richard's welcome-home party. It was all a misunderstanding, Richard claimed, but Glen would bet his last dollar Grady'd never see that money again.

Some time later, when the opportunity presented itself, Glen made his way over to Ellie. Richard was preoccupied singing a jazzed-up version of "Happy Birthday" to Ruth. Glen never did trust a man who craved being the center of attention. Anyone else would have asked Ruth to stand up, would have made *her* the focus. Not Richard. He had everyone gather around him, and it seemed to Glen he treated Ruth's birthday like an afterthought, like a mere pretext for his own performance. Typical. Richard sure hadn't changed.

"Nice party," he said, strolling casually to Ellie's side.

She stood at the edge of the group and Glen was grateful she hadn't taken a front-row seat to Richard's antics. Grady's brother had plenty of other admirers at the moment and seemed to have forgotten his date. Glen, however, resisted pointing this out to Ellie. "Good news about Nell and her dude ranch," he said, instead.

"Sure is," Ellie responded. "I really think she can make it work."

"Yeah. Nell can do it if anyone can."

Ellie nodded. "I haven't seen you in a few days."

"I've been busy."

"Me, too."

"I noticed," he said, thinking about the way she'd cozied up to Richard.

Ellie laughed. "You sound jealous."

"Not me." He raised both hands in a dismissive gesture, then realized she was making an effort to put their relationship back on its previous footing. "But I could be," he said, falling into the easy banter they'd so often exchanged.

"I'm glad to hear it." Her smile was like a splash of sunshine, and Glen felt a rush of relief. She was as determined as he was to forget that stupid kiss. "You're a good friend, Ellie."

"Not as good as I'd hoped."

His heart went still. "What do you mean?"

"You didn't tell me about Bitter End," she accused him, turning to meet his eyes.

"What?" He hadn't been to the ghost town since he was a teenager, and once was enough. There was something dangerous about that place—and he wasn't thinking about the abandoned wells, either.

"Who told you?" he demanded, although the answer was obvious.

"Richard."

"Listen, Ellie," he said, gripping her elbow. He longed to take her by the shoulders and shake some sense into her, but he knew she wouldn't listen and he'd hurt his cause more than help it. "I'd forget about Bitter End if I were you."

"Why should I? This is the most exciting thing I've heard in ages. My father's great-grandparents belonged to the first group of settlers, you know." She paused and studied him. "Glen, what's so bad about this town? Why doesn't anyone talk about it? If you know where it is and other people do, too, why is it a deep dark secret?"

Glen wasn't sure how to explain it to her, especially since he didn't fully understand it himself. All he could remember was the eerie sense of danger and oppressiveness he'd experienced the one and only time he'd been there. He couldn't have been more than fourteen at the time. Cal, Grady and he had inadvertently overheard their parents discussing the old town and decided to locate it on their own. It'd taken them weeks to find it, but instead of feeling a sense of triumph and elation after their first visit, they'd been terrified. They'd hardly spoken of it since.

"I don't want you going there," he ordered, rather than answer her questions. The second those words left his lips, Glen recognized his mistake. Ellie wasn't going to take kindly to anyone telling her what she could or couldn't do.

"Too late. Richard's driving me there tomorrow afternoon."

"No, he's not." Even knowing he was digging himself in deeper didn't prevent Glen from blurting it out.

"You don't have any right to tell me that."

"Ellie, listen to me—"

"I've heard everything I care to hear. I thought we were friends."

"We are," he said, his mind spinning. He realized that the thought of Ellie in that deserted town frightened him. All his protective instincts snapped into place—instincts he'd never associated with Ellie. "I don't want you going there."

"You're being ridiculous. You found it, and now I want to see it, too. It was okay for you, but not for me? I don't accept that, Glen."

"If you value our friendship, you won't go."

Ellie looked at him as though she'd never seen him before, and once again Glen realized he'd said it all wrong. "If you value my opinion..." he altered hurriedly, but he could see it was already too late.

"I don't think I know you any longer," she whispered. It wasn't her words as much as the way she said them, in a hurt voice that vibrated with doubts.

He'd known it was going to happen, had worried about it for days. He just hadn't thought it'd be so soon. That kiss really had ruined everything. Every shred of closeness they'd once shared was gone. They seemed incapable of even the most basic communication.

"Fine," he said, furious with himself and taking it out on her. "Go ahead and do as you like. Just don't say I didn't warn you." Having botched the entire conversation, he whirled around and walked away. Ellie would discover everything she needed to know about Bitter End soon enough. But she wouldn't have him standing guard over her when she did.

"YOU READY?" Richard asked, entering the feed store fifteen minutes past the time they'd agreed to meet.

"As ready as I'll ever be." The argument with Glen weighed heavily on her mind. She'd considered phoning Richard to beg off, but she refused to allow Glen to tell her what to do. She had as much right as anyone else to visit Bitter End.

Richard laughed. "Just remember you're the one who insisted on going." He sang a few bars of the theme song from *Ghostbusters,* and Ellie laughed, too. He certainly seemed to be in high spirits, which helped to reassure her.

Glen, on the other hand, had made it sound as if going to Bitter End meant risking life and limb. While she might have been willing to listen to reason, she'd deeply resented the way he'd spoken to her. He'd given her *orders,* for heaven's sake.

Everything about their short exchange rankled. Ellie felt bad about it herself, wanting their relationship to return to the way it had been before the kiss. She should have

stopped him, should have known anything physical between them would lead to problems. The only reason she'd
let it happen was that she'd been so upset. Glen had regretted it, too; he'd as much as told her.

Richard helped her into the truck, which Ellie realized
was Grady's. His spirits remained high as he drove out of
town, down the two-lane highway.

Suddenly he veered off the road into a rocky meadow
with cedar shrubs and knee-high weeds.

"So this is the way?"

"No," he said. "I just want you to think it is." The
pickup pitched sharply right, one of the front tires slam-
ming against a rock. Ellie was shoved into the door, hitting
her shoulder hard. She yelped in pain.

"Sorry," Richard said, slowing the vehicle. "You
okay?"

"Fine. What about the truck?" She assumed he was
stopping to survey any damage to the wheels, but she was
wrong.

He leaned toward her and opened the glove compart-
ment, removing a black handkerchief.

"What's that?" she asked.

"A blindfold."

"A what?" she exploded.

"Blindfold," he repeated calmly. "I thought about this
carefully and it's the only way I'll agree to take you to
Bitter End."

"You're joking, right?"

"I'm taking you against my better judgment. If Grady
ever found out, he'd have my hide."

"Glen wasn't too pleased about it, either."

"You told him?" Richard's eyes flared with anger.

"Yes, we…we exchanged a few words and left it at
that."

"Tell him you changed your mind."

Ellie stared at Richard in shock. "You want me to lie?"

"Well, not lie...exactly. Just let him assume you followed his advice. Understand?"

"A lie by omission is still a lie."

"Whatever. Just do it." He held up the blindfold.

"I'm not wearing that."

"Then I'm not taking you to Bitter End." The way he said it made her realize he wasn't kidding. The facade vanished, and she viewed a side of Richard she'd never seen before. A side that wasn't cordial or friendly but, rather, dark and menacing.

"I have to wear the blindfold?"

He nodded, then his face relaxed into a boyish grin. "Think of it as a game."

"All right." But she didn't like it, and her dislike intensified when he placed the handkerchief around her eyes, tying it securely at the back of her head.

"Can you see anything?"

"No."

"You're sure?"

"Positive." His repeated questions irritated her.

He started the truck again and pulled back onto the highway. He seemed to be driving around in circles. When he finally did leave the road, she was completely confused and had no idea what direction he'd taken. On the rough off-road terrain, the truck bounced and heaved in every direction.

Ellie lost track of time. It might have been fifteen minutes or an hour, she didn't know. All she knew was that they'd stopped.

"Richard?"

He didn't answer. But she knew immediately that they were close to Bitter End. She *felt* it. A heavy uncomfortable sensation descended on her, a feeling that was completely at odds with the sun's warmth pouring through the windows.

"We're here, aren't we?" she asked.

Silence.

"Richard?"

Silence again.

She heard a soft eerie sound, a creaking that could have been the truck door opening. Or was it something else? Something sinister.

"This is ridiculous," she said, and lifted the blindfold from her eyes. Richard wasn't beside her, nor was he visible from where she sat. Squinting into the sunlight, she climbed out of the truck.

The first thing she saw was a faint footpath leading away from the truck. Not knowing what else to do, she followed it, clambering over rocks and forcing her way through the undergrowth. Soon the town came into sight; she could see it clearly from a limestone outcropping just above. She stopped and stared.

Bitter End was surprisingly intact. A number of buildings, some of them stone, some wood, stood along a main street, which was bordered by a plank walk. A church steeple showed in the distance, charred by fire. She saw a hotel and livery stable with a small corral. Even a building that had apparently been a saloon.

She still couldn't see Richard anywhere.

"Richard!" she called again. "Where are you? If this is a joke I'm not laughing."

She half-slid, half-ran down the incline to the town.

She felt a sudden chill on her bare arms. Although the day was warm and windless, the town was decidedly cold.

"Richard!" she shouted again.

Nothing.

Cautiously she ventured onto the street, but her companion was nowhere to be seen. Panic clawed at her stomach as she spun around. "Richard! For the love of God, where are you?"

Chapter Four

Caroline was busy sorting mail when she heard a customer at the front counter. Because the post office was open only two hours on Saturdays, she often did a brisk business then.

Setting aside the stack of letters, she stepped out to the customer-service area. When she recognized Grady Weston, her posture immediately became defensive; she could feel it. Generally Savannah—and now occasionally Richard—collected the mail for the Yellow Rose Ranch. Grady hadn't been into the post office since last May and he'd come only because he was seeking her help. But then, he'd been worried about Savannah's relationship with Laredo Smith. A relationship he'd tried to destroy. He hadn't trusted Laredo, and he hadn't understood Savannah. In fact, Grady had seriously underestimated both of them.

"Morning, Grady," she said warily. The last time she'd seen him, he'd been laughing hysterically at the prospect of attending Ruth's birthday party with her.

"Caroline." He nodded, looking about uncomfortably. He removed his Stetson and held the brim with both hands.

"Can I help you?" she asked.

He blinked as though someone had lifted him off his horse and hurled him straight into the middle of town. He shook his head in a puzzled way, apparently wondering how he happened to be there in the post office, talking to her.

"Do you need stamps?" she asked.

"No." He shifted his weight from left to right. "I, uh, came for another reason."

She waited impatiently for him to continue. Grady had never been a smooth talker like his brother, but Caroline suspected his hesitation had something to do with their last unfortunate meeting.

"It's about what I said the other day—or what I said that you heard. What I mean to say..." He snapped his jaw closed and she noticed the color creeping up his neck. "Savannah said you weren't really offended, but I can't help feeling that—"

"Don't worry about it," she said, rather than have him endure this embarrassment any longer. "Let's put it behind us."

He relaxed visibly. "That's kind of you. I didn't mean anything by it."

"I know. Savannah shouldn't play matchmaker—she has no talent for it." Caroline was all too aware that her best friend was in love with love. Savannah wanted Caroline to know the same happiness herself but unfortunately was convinced Grady was the man she'd find it with.

Caroline knew she was at fault, too. She should have discouraged Savannah from the first, but deep down part of her had *wanted* Grady to notice her. She liked Grady, perhaps more than she should, seeing that they couldn't even carry on a conversation without arguing about *something.*

"I wouldn't have minded going to Ruth's party with you. I realize I must have sounded like I'd rather pluck chickens, but that isn't so."

Despite his apology, his attitude tweaked her pride.

"You have to admit it was a crazy idea," he said, holding her gaze. "You and me going out together." He seemed to expect some response from her.

"Let's drop it, all right?" She slapped the mail down on the counter and glared at him, not completely understanding her own anger.

He flinched at the sound. "Now what'd I say?" he demanded.

"Nothing."

"Then why are you looking at me like you're madder than hops?"

Caroline shook her head. "You're the only man I know who can apologize with an insult."

"I insulted you?" His jaw went slack with astonishment.

Caroline drew a deep calming breath and held up her right hand. "Let's just say we'll agree to disagree."

He frowned and twisted the rim of his Stetson. "I need to know what we're agreeing to disagree about."

She gave an impatient sigh. The man was completely and utterly obtuse. "You and I both love Savannah," she said with exaggerated slowness. "But when it comes to each other, we don't see eye to eye, which is fine. We don't really need to. I have my life and you have yours. You don't want to go out with me and that's fine, too. Because frankly I'm not all that interested in you, either."

His eyes narrowed. "In other words you're turning me down before I even get a chance to ask you to the Cattlemen's Association dance."

He was asking her to the dance? So *that* was what this was all about.

Now he was the one who was agitated. He gestured with his hand as if he wasn't sure how to continue. "I take the better part of the morning driving into town," he finally managed. "I've got an entire herd of cattle that need tending, but instead, I waste a good part of my day just so I can invite you to a stupid dance. Then before I can even get the words out, you're telling me you'd rather go out with a polecat than with me. Well, if that doesn't beat all." He slammed his hat back on his head with enough force to make her recoil.

"You wanted to ask me to the dance?" she asked, recovering in record time, "and I'm supposed to be grateful?"

"No...yes," he faltered, then ignored the question. "Why else would I drive into town on a Saturday?" Not giving her time to respond, he added, "Cal's right. A woman's nothing but trouble."

Caroline's heart sank. She would have enjoyed attending the biggest dance of the year with him. Instead, she'd ruined any chance she had of stepping onto the dance floor with Grady Weston.

"I told Savannah this wouldn't work," he said with the self-righteous attitude of a man who thinks he's been right all along. "As far as I'm concerned, this is the last time I'm inviting you to any social function in this town. If you want a date you're going to have to ask *me*."

The insinuation that he was the only man who'd ask her out infuriated Caroline. "I don't need you in order to get a date."

"Oh sure, I suppose you're interested in Richard, too."

"Richard? What's he got to do with anything?"

Grady opened and closed his jaw, but apparently decided against explaining. "Never mind. I'm out of here."

Caroline stretched out her hand to stop him, but it was too late. Grady had already turned and was storming out of the post office, leaving the door to slam in his wake.

"My, oh my, what's gotten into that young man?"

For the first time Caroline noticed Edwina and Lily Moorhouse standing in the post-office foyer. Both women continued to dress as if they still spent their days at the front of a classroom. Caroline couldn't remember ever seeing either one in anything but well-pressed shirtwaist dresses. On Sunday mornings and at important social functions, they wore dainty hats with matching purses and spotless white gloves.

Lily, the younger and less talkative of the two, clutched her mail to her breast as if in mortal fear of having Grady rip it from her.

Edwina, who'd never had a problem sharing what was on her mind, was sputtering about "that young man."

"I apologize, ladies," Caroline said. "Grady and I were having a...difference of opinion."

"So it seems." Edwina pinched her lips together, clenching her purse tightly with both hands.

"Are you all right?" Lily asked.

Caroline shook her head, dismissing the older woman's concern. But the encounter had left her more shaken than she cared to admit.

"You like him, don't you?" Lily asked in a soft voice, and reached across the counter to pat Caroline's hand.

Caroline nodded. Yes, she did like Grady—even if they didn't get along—and it was well past time she admitted it. But then, her judgment in men wouldn't exactly earn her any awards. Maggie's father had left her pregnant, and every other romantic relationship in her adult life had ended badly. "I guess some women are better judges of character than me," she said.

"Grady's a fine young man," Lily insisted, apparently over her shock.

"He's got a heart of gold," Edwina agreed. "But if you want my opinion, I think that young man's constipated."

"You think so, sister?" Lily frowned thoughtfully.

"Indeed I do. You be patient with him, Caroline, and he'll come around. Mark my words."

"I couldn't agree with Edwina more," Lily said, brightening somewhat. ''There's nothing wrong with that young man that a large bowl of stewed prunes wouldn't cure.''

''Or Grandpa's cordial.''

''Indeed!''

ELLIE'S HEART hammered in her ears as she stepped backward, slowly edging her way onto the path toward the truck. Richard was still nowhere to be seen.

Glen's warnings about the ghost town echoed in her mind. Even Richard had advised her not to come. She'd been the one to insist on making the trip, certain that Glen, at least, was being overprotective.

What was worse—far worse—was this…sensation, this feeling. It was as though she was being watched. And judged. And…disliked. Her pulse still thundered in her head, gaining volume and intensity. Her feet dragged heavily as she walked. It almost felt as if someone had bound her arms and legs and was slowly tightening the rope, binding her.

All she could think about was escape. But she couldn't leave, couldn't just turn and run. Somehow, someway she had to find out what had happened to Richard. Although every dictate of her heart and mind urged her to get out of there, she couldn't abandon him.

Besides, she hadn't a clue how to find her way back to Promise. She'd have to search this place and—

''*Boo!*''

Ellie screamed and leaped a good three feet off the ground. Richard threw back his head and laughed hilariously, as if her terror was the funniest thing he'd seen in years.

Furious, Ellie clenched her hands into fists and glared at him.

''Hey,'' he said, continuing to chuckle, ''you're the one who claimed not to be afraid of ghosts.''

"Where'd you go?" she demanded, gripping his arm and clinging tightly. She was too frightened to stay angry for long.

"Hey," he repeated softly, "you're really scared, aren't you?"

"You know I am!"

"Sweetheart, it was a joke."

"A stupid one."

"Okay, okay, it probably wasn't the best thing to do, but you were so sure nothing was going to frighten you. Sorry," he said with a casual shrug. "The real danger is letting your imagination run away with you."

Her fingers tensed on his arms. "I don't like this place."

"I told you." He sounded cool and unaffected.

"Don't you feel it?" she asked, studying him.

"Feel what?"

"The...sense of oppression."

He looked at her as if she needed a psychiatrist. "I don't feel anything. Come on, let me show you around. Old as it is, there's still lots to see."

Even though she was curious, Ellie shook her head. "I think we should head back."

"We just got here. Don't you want to check out the mercantile? I actually found some bloated canned goods left on the shelf. Can you believe it? The cash register is there, too. I looked, but there wasn't any money inside."

Did he actually expect there to be cash for his taking? Ellie wondered.

"What happened to the church?" she asked, gesturing toward the small hill at the far end of the main street.

"I didn't go in. Doesn't interest me. Outside looks like it got hit by lightning."

Ellie stared, fascinated despite her fears.

"Come on," Richard urged again, "let's explore."

Ellie realized it wasn't likely she'd come back for a second visit. "Okay, show me the mercantile," she said, uncertain even now that it was a wise thing to do.

"Sure." He took her hand and led her up the two steps to the raised wooden sidewalk. The old boards creaked with their weight, making an eerie inhuman sound. It looked as though the town had been fairly prosperous at one time. A hotel and saloon, a livery stable, a small corral. The sunbleached planks of the boardwalk were bleached and splintered with age, and several sections had rotted through.

"Watch your step," Richard said, and slipped his arm around her waist, holding her unnecessarily close.

"Maybe we should go to the hotel," he whispered suggestively. "Find a room with a bed."

"No, thanks," she murmured.

"Hey, don't be so quick to turn down a good thing. We could have a lot of fun together."

"No, thanks," she said again, her tone reinforcing the message.

"Pity. We could be good together."

Ellie sincerely doubted that.

As Richard opened the door to the mercantile, the hinges squeaked loudly and Ellie shivered. The sensation persisted, the feeling that she was being watched.

The inside of the old store was like something out of a museum. The counter stretched the length of the room, with shelves built behind it. What Richard had said was true; there were several tin cans scattered about. The cans themselves were swollen, their labels faded.

"What happened to make people move fast enough to leave goods behind?" Life was hard in the Old West, and food was often in short supply.

"Who knows?" Apparently Richard didn't find her question of any interest.

The cash register was there, too, the till open. Bramble

weeds littered the floor. Ellie saw a couple of old barrels and a table, but no chairs.

"Okay, we've seen it," she said. "I'm ready to go back."

"You don't want to see anything else?"

"No." Her curiosity was gone and all she wanted now was to escape. Even knowing that her father's great-grandparents had walked these very streets and stepped inside this store wasn't enough to keep her.

"Come on, let's go look at the hotel," Richard urged again. "There's quite a fancy staircase—if you ignore the occasional broken step."

"Richard!" The hotel had to be riddled with danger. If the staircase collapsed or they fell through a damaged floor, heaven only knew how long it'd be before someone found them.

Glen would come. Ellie was genuinely relieved that she'd told at least one other person where she was headed, even if he disapproved. If she did turn up missing, Glen would leave no stone unturned. He'd look for the town until he located it again. Then he'd mount a search-and-rescue effort, enlist everyone's help. He wouldn't rest until he knew exactly what had happened and why. He was that kind of man. That kind of friend.

"I want to check the cemetery," she decided as they left the mercantile.

"The cemetery? As jittery as you are?" Richard said. "Why?"

"I want to look for a grave. A little boy by the name of Edward Abraham Frasier." Since the Bible had given no information about what had caused his death, perhaps a grave marker would.

"All right," Richard agreed, but she could see he wasn't enthusiastic.

The sensation of someone following them grew less in-

tense as they walked toward the outskirts of town. The gate
to the cemetery hung by one hinge.

"Someone's been here recently," Ellie said, stopping
just inside the fenced area. The dirt had been churned recently to plant a rosebush.

"Savannah," Richard said. "She was after some old
roses and replaced the ones she took."

"Savannah's been here?" Ellie wasn't completely surprised. Savannah scoured the highways and byways for old
roses, hoping to find unfamiliar and unusual species. And
replacing the roses she'd removed? Savannah never took
without giving; it was her nature.

"What was the name again?" Richard asked.

"Edward Abraham Frasier." Some of the graves were
marked with wooden crosses that had badly deteriorated
with age. And only a few names were legible on the stone
markers. After a couple of minutes she gave up the effort.

"You done yet?" Richard asked, sounding bored.

"Yeah." While she wished she'd found the grave, she
didn't want to linger in town any longer.

Richard held her hand as they scrambled up the incline,
then followed the rocky path that led to the truck. He
helped her into the cab—obviously charm died hard—and
climbed inside himself. "Put on the blindfold," he instructed her, turning the ignition key.

Ellie complained under her breath. He had nothing to
worry about; she had no intention of returning to Bitter
End. She didn't know what had made her ancestors leave
the town; all she could say was that she didn't blame them.

Once the blindfold was securely in place, Richard put
the truck into gear.

The ride back to Promise was accomplished in half the
time it had taken to drive out. Once again the truck pitched
and bucked over the uneven terrain, leaving Ellie to wonder
how he'd found Bitter End on his own. Of one thing she

was sure—neither Glen nor Cal would have taken him there. Nor would Grady or Savannah. No one she knew would purposely return to Bitter End. She wouldn't. Never again. Glen was right; once was more than enough.

Richard dropped her at the feed store. "Thanks," she said, and was about to open the door and climb out when he stopped her.

"Hey, there's no need to rush, is there?"

She did have work to do. "Well—"

"Don't you want to thank me?" he asked.

"I thought I already had."

"A kiss wouldn't hurt." Without giving her a chance to respond he reached for her shoulders and brought his mouth to hers. Technically it was a kiss, but Ellie experienced none of the warmth or gentleness she had with Glen. None of the surging passion. What Richard classified as a kiss was little more than the touching of lips.

Apparently he wasn't satisfied, either, because he opened his mouth and twisted it over hers. Ellie still felt nothing. Which surprised her, considering how attractive the man was.

Richard released her and smiled. "I'll give you a call soon," he said as though nothing was amiss. "We could have something good together, Ellie. Think about it, all right?"

She stared at him, at a total loss for anything to say. The kiss that had left her cold had somehow convinced him they could become romantically involved.

"You're coming to the Cattlemen's dance with me, right?" he asked, when she finally climbed down from the truck.

"Ah…" She stood with one hand on the door, ready to close it. "I'll let you know for sure, but I don't think so."

Richard's eyes widened with surprise. "But I'll see you there?"

"I...I don't know." She wasn't in the mood for much partying. "Perhaps," she said vaguely.

"In any case I'll see you soon," Richard said cheerfully, and with a jaunty wave drove off.

Ellie walked into the store and George Tucker handed her a pile of pink slips. "Glen Patterson called three times," he muttered in a way that told her he wasn't keen on being her secretary. George's expertise didn't extend to the office.

"Glen phoned?" Her heart reacted immediately.

"Would you kindly put that young man out of his misery?" George asked. "I've got better things to do than answer his questions about you."

Smiling to herself, Ellie headed for her office in the back of the store. Maybe, just maybe, there was some hope that she and Glen could resurrect their friendship, after all.

GLEN HADN'T BEEN worth a plugged nickel all day. Glen and Cal had been out at Cayuse Pasture, which was approximately twelve miles square in size. They were grazing about 400 cows and yearlings there. Even the dogs didn't want anything to do with him, and Glen saw their point. His mood had been murderous all day. Three times he'd left Cal and the other hands to race back to the house so he could call Ellie. His frustration rose each time he was forced to leave a message with George. Now that he was back at the ranch house, he discovered his disposition hadn't improved. The answering machine showed that Ellie hadn't tried to call him back, which meant she was still with Richard in Bitter End. He didn't like it, not one damn bit.

"If you're so concerned about Ellie," Cal said, "why don't you drive into town and find out what happened to her?" Cal himself would be driving into town later for his weekly visit to Billy D's, the local watering hole. Most single ranchers met at Billy D's for a cold beer on Friday and Saturday nights. Then some of them would wander over to the café in the bowling alley or the Chili Pepper for a barbecued steak. Adam Braunfels served up one of the best T-bones in the state. Glen would probably join his brother and friends—after he'd talked to Ellie.

"You're letting a woman mess with your mind, little brother," Cal said with the voice of one who'd been disillusioned by love. He opened the refrigerator and reached for a can of soda. "Take my advice or leave it—that's up to you. But the way I see it, Ellie's already got a ring through your nose."

"The hell she does," Glen argued. Sure, she'd been on his mind, but *only* because he was worried about her and Richard visiting Bitter End.

"I was thinking about moseying into town early," Glen admitted, making light of it.

"Yeah, fine," Cal said with a decided lack of interest. "Why don't you just marry Ellie and be done with it?"

Glen frowned at his brother, but rather than become involved in a pointless argument he tore up the stairs to shower and change.

By the time Glen reached the outskirts of Promise, anger simmered just below the surface. He intended to check in with his friends at Billy D's in a while, but he wouldn't rest easy until he'd spoken to Ellie. He needed to see for himself that she was all right.

When he arrived at the feed store, George Tucker took one look at him and pointed him toward the business office. So Ellie was back, but she hadn't bothered to return his calls.

The door was half-open and Glen saw Ellie sitting at the desk, her fingers flying over calculator buttons. She glanced up when he walked into the room. Under normal circumstances he would have poured himself some coffee. Not this afternoon. At least not yet. He wanted to find out what her mood was like first.

"You went to Bitter End, didn't you," he said quietly. Although he wished she'd taken his advice, his relief that she was safely home overrode any real anger.

"Did you honestly expect me not to?"

"No," he said, knowing his actions the night of Ruth's party had made that impossible.

"I...I wasn't overly impressed with the town," she admitted.

Well, he thought, that was a start in the right direction.

"Why didn't you ever mention it before?" she asked, and he noticed a hurt tone in her voice.

"I never talked about it with anyone." He walked across the room and reached for the coffeepot. "If I'd told you, you would've wanted to see it for yourself—which you did."

"To tell you the truth, I understand why you didn't want me there."

That was what he'd figured. "I was worried about you," he said.

"I know. I talked to Cal a few minutes ago."

Glen frowned. He could just imagine what his brother had said. On second thought he didn't want to know.

"You plan on making a return visit?" he asked, instead, keeping the question light.

"Go back? Not on your life."

"Good." He raised the mug to his lips and took a sip of coffee.

"I think we should talk," Ellie surprised him by saying.

"Talk?" He froze, not sure he liked the sound of this.

She laughed softly, and Glen realized how much he'd missed hearing that. She had a deep rich laugh, unlike a lot of women he knew who had delicate laughs. Ellie's was robust and confident, as if she didn't need to prove her femininity by being reserved. He found her unique in any number of other ways.

"We can try to ignore it, pretend we've forgotten it, but the best way to deal with...what happened is to discuss it."

His eyes held hers. "Are you talking about..." He was having as much trouble saying the word as she was.

"The...kiss." There, she'd said it.

"The kiss," he repeated in low tones, as though this were something dark and dangerous. He was beginning to think it was.

Ellie laughed, and soon he did, too.

"We should acknowledge that we were caught up in a momentary impulse," she suggested primly. "And... Oh, hell, let's just forget it."

Leaning against the edge of her desk, Glen cradled his coffee mug in both hands. "I don't think that'll work."

"Why not?" Ellie stood and replenished her own coffee.

Because they'd been friends all these years, Glen knew exactly what she was doing. What had prompted her sudden burst of activity wasn't a craving for more coffee but an effort not to let him see what was in her eyes.

He set his mug aside and touched her shoulder. She jerked around as though he'd burned her.

"I don't want to forget the kiss," he said with blinding honesty. He didn't recognize it as the truth until the words left his lips.

"You don't?" She sounded startled.

"Do you?" He was a fool to ask, but he couldn't have held back the question for anything.

"I...I don't know."

"Yes, you do." If he could hang out his pride to dry, then she'd damn well better be prepared to do the same thing.

She blinked twice. "All I want is for us to be friends."

"We are. That hasn't changed."

"But it *has!*" she cried, gesturing wildly with her hands. "That kiss changed everything. I used to be able to talk to you."

"You still can."

"No, I can't."

"Try me," he challenged.

She threw back her head and laughed, but this time her amusement lacked sincerity. "We can talk about anything, can we?" she flung at him. "Fine, then we'll talk about how Richard's kisses leave me cold and how all I could do was compare the way I felt when I was in your arms."

Glen didn't hear anything beyond the first few words. "So you're kissing Richard now. Is there anyone else I don't know about?"

"See?" she cried, tossing her arms in the air. "My point exactly."

"What point?"

"We can't talk."

"We're already talking! What do you mean?" This was the kind of convoluted conversation women suckered a man into—giving him just enough rope to hang himself. Glen had seen it happen often enough and had always managed to avoid it with Ellie. Until now.

"You said there wasn't anything I couldn't discuss with you, and already we're at each other's throats."

"I am not at your throat!" he shouted, his patience gone. The entire day had been a waste. First he'd fretted about her with Richard in Bitter End. Then he'd attempted to revive their friendship, only to learn she'd been locking lips with Richard Weston.

"You're welcome to him," he said, setting the mug down forcibly enough to send coffee sloshing over the sides. "As far as I'm concerned, you and Richard deserve each other."

"Oh, please, now you're acting like a jealous fool."

He was out the office door before he realized he'd had more than one reason for seeing Ellie. He walked back and leaned against the doorjamb, crossing his arms.

Ellie glanced up and waited.

"You going to the dance?" he asked finally, as if her answer didn't really matter.

"I...haven't decided yet. Are you going?"

"Yeah."

"Then I probably will, too."

"See you there?" he asked, his mood brightening.

She nodded. "Will you wait for me?"

He nodded, grinning.

She smiled back.

Chapter Five

As the evening wore on, Glen's feelings toward Richard Weston grew even less friendly. He resented the other man's putting Ellie at risk by escorting her to Bitter End. The more he thought about it, the more irritated he got. Richard's dating Ellie had never set right with him, either. Especially now, when she was at a low point in her life following her father's death and her mother's move to Chicago. Although Ellie generally had a level head, Glen didn't want Pretty Boy taking advantage of her.

And then there was his own unresolved—and unexpected—attraction to her.... But no, the real concern was Ellie's vulnerability to a superficial charmer like Richard.

The only thing to do, Glen decided, was speak to Richard personally. Clear the air. Set him straight. He'd wait for the right opportunity. He was well aware that Ellie wouldn't appreciate his having a chat with Richard on her behalf, but she didn't need to know about it, either. Someone had to look after her interests. Glen liked to think of himself as her guardian. Okay, *guardian* was probably the wrong word, seeing as they were close to the same age. What she could use was a sort of...advocate. A concerned friend. Yes, that was it. An advocate. Someone who had her best interests at heart. Stepping in where needed.

With his role clear in his mind, he held off until late

Wednesday afternoon before driving out to the Yellow Rose Ranch and confronting the youngest Weston. This was between him and Richard. Man to man.

He turned into the drive and parked in the yard beside Grady's truck, then slowly climbed out of the cab. Savannah was in her rose garden wearing a wide-brimmed straw hat to shield her face from the sun. Richard sat on the front porch, strumming a guitar, apparently so involved in his music that he didn't see or hear Glen's approach. Rocket, Grady's old black Lab, slept on the porch, sprawled out on a small braided rug.

Carrying a wicker basket filed with fragrant pink roses, Savannah waved and walked toward Glen.

"Howdy, neighbor," she said, smiling her welcome.

"Savannah." He touched the tip of his Stetson. "Beautiful day, isn't it?"

"Lovely," she agreed.

"I'm here to see Richard," Glen announced, narrowing his gaze on the man who still lounged on the porch.

"He's practicing his guitar." She gestured unnecessarily toward Richard. He'd leaned the chair against the side of the house and propped one foot on the porch railing.

"Would you care for a glass of iced tea?" Savannah offered.

His throat was dry; something cold and wet would be appreciated. "That's mighty kind of you."

Richard's sister moved toward the house, then paused at the bottom step and turned. With a slight frown she said, "Is there trouble, Glen? Between you and Richard?"

"Not at all," he was quick to assure her. He was determined that this would look like nothing more than a friendly conversation between neighbors. And if he just happened to mention Ellie...

Obviously relieved, Savannah disappeared into the house, and Glen approached Richard. The younger man ignored him until Glen pulled at the chair beside his and plunked himself down.

Richard's fingers paused over the strings. "Howdy, Glen."

"Howdy." Although Glen had mulled over what he intended to say, he found that actually speaking his mind was surprisingly difficult. "Do you have a few minutes?"

"Sure." Richard set the guitar down on the porch, holding it by the neck. "I've always got time for a friend."

Friend. Glen hesitated, since he didn't exactly view Richard that way.

"What can I do for you?" Richard asked companionably.

"Well…" Nope, he wasn't very good at expressing himself, Glen thought. "I've been concerned about Ellie."

"Really?" Richard asked. "Why?"

"Her father dying and then her mother leaving so soon afterward."

Richard nodded. "I see what you mean. She seems to be handling it pretty well, though, don't you think?" He picked up the guitar, laid it across his lap and played a couple of chords.

"That's the thing about Ellie," Glen explained, speaking with authority. After all, he knew Ellie far better than Richard did. "She can put on a good front, but there's a lot of emotion churning beneath the surface."

Richard chuckled. "You're right about that! She's a little fireball just waiting to explode. I've always been attracted to passionate women." His tone insinuated that he'd been close to getting scorched by Ellie a few times—as if he knew her in ways Glen never would.

Glen shifted uncomfortably, angered by the insinuation, but was saved from responding by Savannah, who carried out a tray with two tall glasses of iced tea and a plate of homemade oatmeal cookies.

"Thanks," Glen said, accepting a glass.

Richard had reached for his, plus a cookie, before Savannah could even put the plate down. "I can never resist my sister's cookies," he said, and kissed her on the cheek. "No one bakes better cookies than Savannah."

His sister smiled at his praise, then quietly returned to the kitchen. Glen watched her go, and realized that with very little effort, Richard had won over Savannah, too—despite all the grief he'd brought the family. No doubt about it, the guy was an expert when it came to manipulating women. Glen felt all the more uneasy, wondering how to handle the situation. He wanted Richard to keep his distance from Ellie, but he didn't want to be obvious about it. If he made a point of warning Richard off, the bum would be sure to tell her what he'd said. Probably snicker at him, too.

The best way, he decided, was to state his concerns in a natural straightforward manner. "Ellie told me you took her to Bitter End," he began, struggling to disguise his anger.

Richard threw back his head and laughed boisterously. "I scared the living daylights out of her, too."

Glen hadn't heard about that and was forced to listen to Richard's story of how he'd blindfolded her, then slipped out of the truck and hidden.

By the time he finished, Glen's jaw hurt from the effort it took not to yell at the man. "I don't think it's a good idea to be taking anyone up to that ghost town," he said as calmly as he could, realizing anew that he actively disliked Richard Weston. He hadn't cared for him as a teenager and liked him even less as an adult.

"I couldn't agree with you more," Richard said, once his amusement had faded. "It was a mistake to even mention Bitter End. Once I did, she was all over me, wanting to see the place. When I finally said I'd take her, she wasn't in the town five minutes before she wanted to leave.

"Surprising how much of that town's still standing," Richard said next, helping himself to a second cookie.

Glen figured if he didn't take one soon, Richard would devour the entire plateful before he'd even had a taste. Deliberately he reached for a cookie, then another. He took a bite; they *were* as good as Richard claimed.

"How'd you find the town?" Glen asked.

"Since you, Cal and Grady didn't see fit to include me when we were kids, I didn't have any choice but to seek it out on my own."

"But why now?"

"Why not?" He shrugged as if it was of little consequence. "I've got plenty of time to kill while I wait to hear on my next job. I work for an investment company."

"I didn't realize that."

"I don't tell a lot of people," he said. "Most recently I was working with a smaller institution, specializing in loans and investments. Unfortunately, as you're probably aware, the larger institutions are swallowing up the smaller ones, and I was forced to take a short vacation while the company reorganizes. It seemed as good a time as any to visit my family."

"Investments? Really?" Richard certainly possessed the polished look of a professional. And he knew how to talk the talk. Glen was a bit confused, though; he'd been under the impression that Richard had a different sort of job— sales or something. Oh, well, he supposed it didn't matter.

"Yup." Richard ran the guitar pick over the strings and laughed easily. "I bet you didn't know I'd made a quite a name for myself, did you?"

Glen sobered when he realized how smoothly Richard had diverted him from the subject of Bitter End, but he wasn't going to allow the other man to get away with it for long.

"You won't be taking Ellie back to the ghost town, will you?" Glen asked in a tone that told Richard he was in for a fight if he did.

"Not likely!"

"Good." Then, in case he might consider showing the town to others, Glen added, "Or anyone else?"

"Hardly." Richard's response was immediate; but Glen noted the way his hand stilled momentarily over the guitar. "I wouldn't have taken Ellie, but like I said, once I mentioned it she was all over me, wanting to see the place. It was either drive her there myself or let her go looking for it on her own."

That much was true, Glen conceded.

"Do you and Ellie have something going...romantically?" Richard surprised him with the directness of the question.

Glen hesitated, unsure how to respond. Before he allowed himself to confess what he'd denied to everyone, including himself, he shook his head. "We're just friends."

"That's what I thought." Richard sounded smug and satisfied.

"Any particular reason you're asking?"

"Yeah. I'm interested in her myself, and I don't want to step on your toes if I can help it."

Glen frowned. "Like I said earlier, this is a bad time for Ellie."

"She needs someone like me," Richard said, bending over the guitar and tightening a couple of strings. "What I'd like to see her do is sell that business and get on with her life. Her daddy stuck her with that feed store, but there's no need for her to hold on to it."

Glen shook his head. Ellie loved the store with the same intensity her father had. She recognized her contribution to the community and took pride in meeting the needs of the local ranchers. The feed store had become the unofficial gathering place in town, and that was because Ellie, like her father, made folks feel welcome.

Everyone dropped in at Frasier Feed, to visit, catch up on local news and gossip, swap stories. The large bulletin board out front offered free advertising space for anyone with something to trade or sell. The pop machine was there, too, with a couple of chairs for those who wanted to take a load off their feet.

Ellie sell out? Never. Apparently Richard didn't know her as well as he thought.

"She's interested in me, too, you know," Richard added.

This definitely came as surprise to Glen. She'd admitted the two of them had kissed, but in the same breath had told him she preferred his kiss over Richard's. At least, that was what he *thought* she'd said. The last part of their conversation had been lost on him. They'd snapped at each other, gotten annoyed with each other and instantly regretted it. Glen had come to mend fences with her, not destroy them, and he'd turned back to ask her about the dance. He'd made it clear that he looked forward to spending the evening with her.

She'd told him basically the same thing. They'd meet there. He'd wait for her.

"She's attending the dance with me," Richard stated nonchalantly.

"With you?" Glen couldn't believe what he'd just heard. "The Cattlemen's Association dance?"

"Yeah. She had some concern about the two of us being there together, though. Neither of us wants to start any talk."

"Talk?"

"About seeing one another exclusively."

"I see." Glen's hand tensed around the cold glass.

"You going?" Richard asked pointedly. "If I remember correctly, this dance is one of the biggest social events of the summer."

"I'll probably be there," Glen said. And he'd make damn sure Richard kept his paws where they belonged, because the first time he saw Mr. Investment Manager touching Ellie, Glen would be dragging him outside and rearranging his dental work. Even if Ellie *did* prefer Weston, as it now appeared.

"Who are you taking?" Richard probed.

"I...don't know yet," Glen confessed, and then because he didn't want it to look like he couldn't get a date, he added, "I was thinking of asking Nell Bishop."

"Sure," Richard said with an approving nod. "Ask Nell. I bet she'd be happy to go with you."

Glen gulped down the rest of his tea and stood. "Glad we had this conversation," he said, when in reality he was anything but. Only this time his anger was directed at Ellie. She'd played him for a fool. A fool! She'd led him to believe she didn't have a date. Moreover she'd indicted in no uncertain terms that she'd welcome his company there. *Wait for me,* she'd said.

What she intended, he now realized, was that he'd arrive and then stand there twiddling his thumbs while she danced her way across the room in Richard Weston's arms. Well, if that didn't beat all. The why of it wasn't too clear, but he figured Ellie was still mad at him and this was her revenge.

"Don't be a stranger," Richard said as Glen started toward his truck. "And don't worry about me taking Ellie up to Bitter End again, either."

"I won't." He wouldn't worry about a lot of things concerning Ellie, he mused, his anger festering. If it wasn't for Richard letting slip that she'd agreed to be his date, Glen would have arrived at the dance completely unawares.

Maybe Cal was right. Maybe women *couldn't* be trusted.

FRANK HENNESSEY had been the duly elected sheriff of Promise for near twenty years. He knew everyone in town and they knew him. Because he'd been in office for so long, folks were comfortable coming to him with their problems. Minor ones and ones that weren't so minor. Sometimes he suggested they talk to Wade McMillen, the local preacher, and other times he just listened. Mostly folks felt better after they'd talked. More often than not a solution would present itself, although he'd barely say a word. Then folks would credit him when the answer had been there all along buried deep within themselves.

These days Frank had been hearing a lot about Richard Weston. Not that it surprised him. He knew Richard had absconded with the family inheritance the day Grady and Savannah had lowered their parents into the ground. Many a night he'd sat with Grady while the young man grappled with what to do—whether to press charges or not. In the end he'd decided not to pursue a case against Richard, but it had taken Grady damn near six years of constant struggle to work his way out of the red.

Now Richard was back, and Frank had heard from two or three of the local merchants that he was running up charges and not paying his bills. Frank didn't like the sound of this. What to do about it had weighed heavily on his mind for a couple of days.

He'd urged Max Jordan from Jordan's Town and Country outfitters to mention the bill to Grady, but Max didn't want to carry tales to Richard's big brother. Besides, he'd sold two vests like the one Richard had bought after he'd worn his about town. Frank would say one thing about the youngest Weston: he was a real clotheshorse. Max said he'd moved some other high-end clothing items because of

Richard and was therefore willing to cut the young Weston a little slack.

For the moment, Millie Greenville was amenable about the money Richard owed her, as well. Grady had ended up paying for the flowers Richard had bought for his party; Frank knew that and had his doubts as to whether Grady would ever be repaid. Although Richard was already two months past due in paying her for the flowers he'd ordered since, she'd decided not to press the issue. He'd sent a huge arrangement for John Frasier's funeral and a number of other small bouquets to women around town. According to Milly, Richard had apologized and given her a plausible excuse; she'd chosen to believe him. But it was a little worrisome having four hundred dollars outstanding at the end of the month, all owed by the same customer.

Then there was the matter of the tab Richard was running at Billy D's. Apparently Richard had been more than generous about buying other people's drinks. It wasn't unusual for him to order a round for his friends and their friends, too, and then tell Billy just to add it to his tab. When Billy mentioned it to Frank, the money owed was close to five hundred dollars. Richard had fed the tavern owner some cockeyed story about being an investment broker, expecting a commission check that was due any day. Again Billy was willing to wait, seeing as Richard always drew a crowd. He was clever and amusing and people seemed to enjoy themselves when he was around.

Frank looked at his watch and eagerly shoved back his chair. "I'll be over at Dovie's," he said to his deputy on his way out the door. Ever since Dovie had opened her Victorian Tea Room, he stopped by each afternoon around four-thirty, after she'd finished serving tea and scones. The store was generally quiet then, and she'd usually offer him something to satisfy his sweet tooth.

Dovie was his friend. His *special* friend. If it was up to

her, they'd be married, but Frank wasn't the marrying kind. He had no interest in giving up his freedom, although if any woman could tempt him to relinquish his bachelor status, it'd be Dovie. They'd been dating more than ten years now, and about once a year she got uppity about the absence of an engagement ring. Frankly he liked their arrangement just the way it was, and if pressed, Dovie, he suspected, would admit she did, too. Twice a week he spent the night at her house—the two best nights of the week. No, he figured, this marriage business was a token protest on her part. The situation was ideal for both of them as it stood; Dovie liked her freedom as much as Frank liked his, and this way they enjoyed the benefits of a steady relationship. Best of both worlds.

Frank entered the antique shop and once again admired how Dovie had artfully arranged five tables in the corner of her compact store. To his relief, the tea room was empty, and he hoped she'd take a few minutes to sit down and chat with him.

"Afternoon, Dovie," he said, pulling out a chair at his favorite table. She'd done the shop up all fancy. Real elegant. The tea room, too. All the tablecloths and matching napkins were good linen, and tea was served on a china service with sterling silver.

Frank was impressed by Dovie's creative style. She'd taken several bulky pieces of heavy antique furniture—dressers and wardrobes and the like—and used them to display her goods. She positioned things attractively: fringed silk scarves dangled from open drawers, as did long jet necklaces of 1920s vintage. Linens and lace doilies, and large hats with feather plumes and nets sat on shelves. Mismatched antique china, porcelain oil lamps, silver candelabra—she had knickknacks everywhere. Pricey ones, too. Dovie didn't sell junk; she sold *treasures*. She made sure he understood that. Far be it from him to question such matters.

Frank had never seen a woman more in love with things. Every square inch of the shop was used for display. The ladies in town loved to browse there. Most men were afraid to move a foot inside for fear they'd knock something down and end up paying for it.

Dovie looked up from tallying her receipts to send Frank a welcoming smile. As always, it made his heart beat a little faster. He returned the smile and settled back to wait.

When she was finished, Dovie poured him a cup of coffee and brought it, with a slice of warm apple crisp, to the table. Actually he'd been looking forward to her bread pudding with brandy sauce, but since he never paid for these treats, he could hardly complain.

"You look like you've been busy," he said.

"I have." She took the chair across from him, removed her shoes and rubbed her tired feet. "Ellie Frasier was in and bought the Gibson-girl dress for the dance. My, she looked lovely. I know it was more than she wanted to spend, but once she tried it on, she was sold. I don't think I appreciated what a pretty young woman she is," Dovie said absently.

Frank sneaked a peek at Dovie's ankle. She had a fine pair of legs. He'd always been taken with her trim ankles, and never had understood why she insisted on wearing long dresses. It was criminal the way she hid those shapely legs of hers.

One bite of the apple crisp and Frank closed his eyes, savoring the combination of tart and sweet flavors.

"Good?" she asked, even though Frank was sure she already knew it was.

"Excellent."

He ate the rest of it in record time.

"You've got something on your mind, Frank," Dovie said. "I can always tell. Are you going to say what it is?"

"Someone's going around charging a lot of money with local merchants," he told her reluctantly. "I'm not convinced he's planning to pay off his debts."

"Someone?" Dovie repeated. "You don't need to say who. I can guess."

He'd already said more than he should have, so he left it at that. He trusted Dovie. She wasn't like some women who just couldn't keep anything to themselves. He'd never known her to break confidences or spread rumors. It was one of the many things he valued about her.

"What are you going to do about it?"

"I don't know that I *can* do anything. He hasn't broken any laws."

"True," she said, looking thoughtful. "But you might have a chat with him. Man to man—or rather, sheriff to miscreant. I recall you had plenty to say to Laredo Smith not long ago."

Frank ignored the comment about his talk with Laredo, especially since he regretted having said a word. He'd made one mistake in judging character recently and didn't want to make another. He couldn't be one-hundred percent sure, after all, that Richard *didn't* have money coming in.

"I don't know what I could say to this guy." Frank didn't have any right to question Richard about his financial affairs.

"Frank, a lot of small businesses can't afford to take losses. Some months it's all we can do to pay the rent, let alone make a living wage. Let him know you're on to him."

"But he hasn't done anything that warrants my speaking to him."

"He doesn't know that. Let him think you have plenty of reasons. Put the fear of God into him before he robs the entire community blind," she urged. "Before he puts one of us out of business."

Frank knew how close to the edge some businesses operated. Dovie herself wasn't going to get rich with her antique shop, although it was one of the most popular stores in town.

"If nothing else," Dovie added, "it might make him think twice before charging something again."

"True." Frank rubbed his chin. It wasn't his place to tell shop owners who they should extend credit to and who they should avoid, but he hated the thought of Richard's taking advantage of good honest folk.

Dovie drank a little more of her coffee, then carried the china cup to the small kitchen in the back room. Frank followed her with his empty cup and plate.

"You need someone to help you out here now you've got the tea room," he said. It was clear to him she was working far too many hours, and while he'd encouraged her to add the Victorian Tea Room, he was concerned about the toll these extra hours took. The fatigue, the lack of private time.

"You're right, I could use another pair of hands," she said. "But I can't afford to put anyone on the payroll just yet."

Frank slipped his arms around her waist. "I guess you've picked out something special to wear to the dance," he said, nuzzling her neck. "I'm going to be the envy of every man there."

"You've been kissing the Blarney stone again, haven't you?" Dovie teased.

"The only thing I'm interested in kissing is the widow Boyd." Not giving her time to object, he turned her in his arms and brought her mouth to his. She was soft and warm and her gentle kisses fired his blood to life.

"Frank," she whispered, breaking off the kiss. She

looked flustered, her face red and her hands flying around her head checking that her hair was still tucked in place. "For the love of Ireland, it's the middle of the afternoon! Anyone could walk in."

"Let them."

"You're getting mighty bold, Mr. Sheriff." Her eyes narrowed slightly. "Are you ready to take the leap yet?"

Marriage. She hadn't mentioned it in nearly a year. Her question had the effect of a bucket of cold water dumped on his head. His discomfiture must have shown in his face, because Dovie giggled and quickly kissed his jaw.

"You'd better go now," she said good-spiritedly.

"I've got to talk to a certain young man," he said. But he stole another kiss on his way out the door.

THE ANTIQUE WHITE cotton-lawn dress, lavishly trimmed in lace, was quite possibly the most beautiful dress Ellie had ever owned. She hadn't intended to buy it. But every time she walked past the window of Dovie's store, she'd stopped and admired it. On impulse she'd decided to examine it up close. It was fate, she told herself. Fate. First of all the dress was her size, and when she tried it on, it fit like a dream. The moment she saw her reflection in Dovie's mirror, she knew she had to have it for the dance.

Perhaps she was putting too much stock in what Glen had said. He hadn't formally asked her to the dance, but he'd told her he'd be there. He'd also let her know he'd be waiting for her to arrive.

It was *almost* a date. She and Glen. Every time she thought about it, a warm feeling came over her. She and Glen together. Dancing. Kissing. A couple.

Her stomach fluttered and she pressed her hand over it, closing her eyes. So much had happened in the past few weeks. For a while, after her father's funeral and her mother's move to Chicago, Ellie had felt alone. Abandoned and unloved. She didn't feel that way now.

She realized that a lot of her new optimism was because of her changing relationship with Glen. If he'd stayed a little longer the last time he was in the store, they would've kissed again. All her instincts told her that. What surprised her was that she wouldn't have minded. In fact, just the opposite.

Maybe friends did make the best lovers, which she'd heard and read for years. She'd never thought of Glen in those terms before, but now she was ready to move on to a different kind of relationship with him—a romantic one. She thought he was, too. And if he had any doubts about his feelings, the moment he saw her in that dress his mind would be made up.

She grinned when she thought how smart a saleswoman Dovie was. If the woman had gushed all over her when she tried on the dress, she might not have purchased it. Instead, all Dovie had done was smile and escort Ellie to the full-length mirror.

Dovie didn't need to sell the dress; the dress had sold itself.

Ellie ran her hand down the sleeve one last time, then shut the office door. Tonight she'd take it home, hang it in her closet and look forward to Saturday the way a high-school junior anticipates her first prom. She could hardly wait to see Glen's reaction.

Near closing time Nell Bishop showed up with a list of needed supplies.

"I had a wonderful time at Ruth's party," Ellie told her as she looked over the list.

"Ruth's still talking about it," Nell said.

"And I think it's great you're going to start a dude ranch."

"Well, I don't have any takers yet."

"But you will." Ellie was sure of that.

"Are you going to the dance?" Nell asked suddenly.

Ellie smiled; the Cattlemen's Association summer dance appeared to be on everyone's mind. "I didn't think I would at first but...I had a change of heart. So I'll be there. What about you?"

Nell shook her head. "I don't know..."

Ellie understood Nell's indecision. While almost everyone came with a date, it wasn't necessary. Technically she herself was attending the function dateless.

"You don't need to worry if you don't have an escort," Ellie assured her, and was about to explain her own situation when Nell continued.

"It's not that." She wore a puzzled frown. "I'm just wondering if there's something in the air, because I received two invitations in one hour."

It was time the men in this town woke up and realized what a wonderful woman Nell Bishop was. "That's great!"

"First Grady Weston phoned. Now, I like Grady, don't get me wrong, but I've always thought of him as..." Again she hesitated, as if unsure what to say next. "I just don't see Grady and me as a couple. If he's going to ask anyone, it should be Caroline Daniels. Those two are perfect for each other."

So Ellie wasn't the only one who'd noticed. "I've always wondered what's kept them apart."

Nell shook her head. "I can't figure it out."

"Do you think it's Maggie?" Ellie asked, referring to Caroline's five-year-old daughter.

"I can't imagine why."

"I don't think Grady's comfortable with kids," Ellie said. She tried to remember seeing Grady with children and couldn't recall a time she had.

"Maybe, but I've got kids, too. In fact, he chatted with

Jeremy for a couple of minutes first. Then when I got on the phone…he invited me.''

"What did you tell him?"

Nell shrugged. "I didn't know what to say. No one's asked me out since Jake died, and I got so flustered I don't know if I made sense. I think I asked him to give me some time to think about it. He agreed."

"I like Grady," Ellie murmured. He wasn't an easy man to know, but he was fair and honest and hardworking.

"I'd no sooner recovered from that when I got another call," Nell said. "It was Glen Patterson."

Glen's name came out of the blue like a flash of lightning. "Glen?" Ellie repeated, the name buzzing in her ear. "Did you say Glen Patterson?"

"Yes. If Grady's invitation surprised me, Glen's knocked me for a loop." She laughed softly. "I think I must have done a fairly good imitation of a guppie. All I could do was open and close my mouth."

The fluttery sensation was back in the pit of Ellie's stomach, only this time it resembled nausea rather than happy anticipation. Ellie had assumed—*believed*—that Glen had wanted her to be his date.

"So you're going to the dance with Glen," Ellie said bluntly, struggling to hide her feelings.

"No. I told him the same thing I told Grady."

"Maybe you should go with both of them. Dangle one on each arm," Ellie suggested, trying for a lighthearted response.

Nell laughed. "Maybe I should. That'd really turn some heads, wouldn't it?"

Somehow Ellie managed a smile. The dress was going back to Dovie's that very afternoon. She'd been an idiot to spend that much money trying to impress a man who'd already approached another woman. Perhaps he thought he'd walk into the Grange Hall with a woman on each of *his* arms. Well, in that case, Glen Patterson had another think coming.

"There's a problem with Glen, though," Nell said, studying Ellie.

"What's that?" she asked, feigning interest.

"It's similar to the one I have with Grady. I always thought you and Glen would make a wonderful couple."

"Glen and me?" Ellie laughed as though it was the funniest thing she'd heard in weeks. "Nah, we're nothing more than friends. If you want to go to the dance with him, don't let me stand in your way. He asked *you*, didn't he?"

"Yes, but—"

"Don't worry about it," Ellie said, surprised how convincing she sounded. "It's no big deal."

"You're sure?"

"Absolutely."

On second thought, Ellie mused, as she rang up Nell's purchases, she was keeping the dress. Not only that, she'd be dancing every dance.

And she hoped Glen got a really good look at her, wearing her beautiful dress and dancing with every attractive single man who asked.

He could eat his heart out!

Chapter Six

This was bound to be an interesting evening, Cal Patterson thought. He climbed into his truck wearing fresh-washed Wrangler's, a string tie and polished boots. The big dance. Which meant there should be lots of entertaining activity as men and women of all ages flirted outrageously; making fools of themselves and each other. A few romances were always made at this kind of event, and a few broken. Yup, it was fascinating to watch, all right, especially if you were a disinterested observer. Like him.

But not like Glen.

Cal wasn't sure where Glen had gone Wednesday afternoon, but his brother had returned in one hell of a mood. While he might not know the particulars, Cal would wager a case of beer that his brother's rotten mood involved Ellie Frasier.

When Cal had made the mistake of mentioning Ellie in connection with the big dance, Glen had all but exploded. Even before Cal could ask any questions, Glen had slammed out the door, but not without dropping a couple of hints first. If Cal guessed right, Ellie had decided to accept Richard Weston's invitation over Glen's.

While her choice surprised him, Cal was the first to admit that women were inconstant creatures who rarely knew their own minds. Best to keep your distance. Next thing

Cal knew, his little brother had asked Nell Bishop; it hadn't done Glen's ego any good when she'd turned him down, too.

Cal himself had been fool enough to let one woman kick him in the gut and had found the experience as painful as anything he'd ever known. By God, he wasn't about to let it happen a second time. Glen, however, seemed destined to learn this particular lesson on his own.

Apparently his younger brother was a slow learner, because tonight he'd come downstairs in a new denim blazer and a pair of blue jeans so crisp they squeaked. His boots were polished to a gloss. One look dared Cal to comment.

He didn't, but he could tell it wasn't dancing that interested Glen. His brother intended to prove to Ellie, and quite possibly himself, that he didn't need her to have a good time. In other words, he was determined to act like a world-class idiot in front of the entire town.

Cal could almost guarantee that before the end of this night, Glen was going to do something really stupid. Now, that would have some entertainment value, but more important, Cal considered it his brotherly duty to be there to pick up the pieces afterward. He felt for Glen; he'd been through this, too. Heartbroken and humiliated.

Oh, yeah, *definitely* best to keep your distance from women.

Cal heard the band playing when he parked his truck in a long line of vehicles outside the Grange Hall. Cars and trucks were crammed bumper to bumper on both sides of the two-lane highway; obviously the parking lot had filled early in the evening. From the look of things everyone in town had shown up for the dance that traditionally kicked off summer.

The piercing strains of a fiddle cut into the night, followed by a banjo and Pete Hadley's melodic voice. Light spilled out of the open doorway and Cal could see a number of the married men clustered outside for a breath of fresh air. That, and a swallow or two of the hard stuff. Cal wasn't much of a drinking man himself. A cold beer now and again was more to his liking.

Someone shouted a greeting and Cal raised his arm in silent salute, but didn't stop to chat. He'd given his brother two hours—two hours during which he'd have his pride booted to hell and gone. If all went according to his calculations, Glen would be drunk soon or wish he was. Give him another hour. At that point Cal would step forward and haul him home.

The poor guy was in love, and while that alone guaranteed disaster, the worst of it was that Glen refused to admit it. Seeing his brother in such sad shape was akin to looking back two years and remembering the way he'd been with Jennifer. It amazed him now he hadn't seen her for what she was. He'd been so deeply infatuated with her he would have done anything to make her happy. Anything to prove how much he cared.

He'd asked her to be his wife, and six months later she'd humiliated him by canceling their wedding at the last minute. All because he wouldn't give up ranching and move to San Antonio or Houston. Jennifer, who'd transferred from Phoenix, Arizona, to take a short-lived job as an assistant bank manager, had wanted out of small-town America. She'd wanted to move him to a city so crowded he'd never be able to breathe.

Cal had loved Jennifer, but he couldn't change who he was, not even for her. When he wouldn't dance to her tune, she pulled out of the wedding only two days before the event. Then she'd skipped town, leaving him to deal with the explanations and the embarrassment. Last he'd heard, Jennifer was living in Houston with some salesman.

He should have realized from the first she was a city girl at heart. But, like Glen, he'd been in love and hadn't recognized what was right there in front of him. Pushing thoughts of his ex-fiancée from his mind, he headed toward the hall.

The huge room was packed, forcing Cal to twist and turn as he made his way through the crowd. Men and women stretched across the hardwood floor in long rows, line dancing to the "Boot-scootin' Boogie." He remembered a few steps himself; Jennifer had insisted he learn the basics, despite the fact that he'd been born with two left feet.

When that song was over, the couples dancing started. Cal peered around, looking for Glen, and finally spotted him. His brother stood on the opposite side of the room, leaning against the bar, his narrowed gaze trained on the dancers. It didn't take a genius to figure out who held his attention.

Ellie.

Cal's eyebrows arched when he saw the object of his brother's affection. He'd never seen Ellie look prettier. The dress wasn't one with a Western flavor, which appeared to be the popular choice, but more old-fashioned. Elegant. She looked *damn* pretty, and Glen wasn't the only one who'd noticed, either.

Richard Weston had his arm tightly wrapped around Ellie's waist. From all appearances they were deeply involved with each other. This was worse than Cal had expected. He knew the type of man Richard Weston was, and he'd figured Ellie would've caught on fast enough herself. Apparently he'd overestimated her ability to judge character. It was a shame, too, because Richard was a user.

This protective feeling toward Ellie surprised Cal. He didn't want to have *any* feelings toward women. Whatever you did, you got your teeth kicked in. Wasn't worth it. Nosiree, he'd learned his lesson the hard way.

As he looked back at his brother, his eyes strayed to the woman standing directly to Glen's left. It took him a moment to remember who she was. The new doc. The first time he'd noticed her she'd worn a power business suit to a barbecue; now she was dressed in jeans and a snap-button Western shirt. Not exactly appropriate attire for the year's most formal event. Cal couldn't help feeling sorry for her, even if she *was* a city girl, but suspected she found this hick-town dance highly amusing. He could picture her phoning her city friends and making fun of the way people dressed and talked in Texas.

The doc must have sensed his scrutiny because she glanced across the room and looked squarely back at him. He glared in her direction, wanting her to know that he didn't like her attitude—or what he assumed her attitude to be.

The music ended just then, and before Cal could stop him, Glen marched onto the dance floor and headed straight for Ellie.

THIS WAS WORKING OUT even better than Ellie had hoped. Glen hadn't been able to take his eyes off her all evening. Richard viewed Glen as competition. She was well aware that his attentions had more to do with one-upmanship than any real interest in her; nevertheless she found flattery a balm to her wounded pride. She knew it was a superficial and childish reaction, but she couldn't help it. Glen had really hurt her by asking Nell to the dance. Temporarily, at least, being with Richard was a way of assuaging that pain.

The one bad side effect was that Glen's presence had brought out a possessiveness in Richard she wasn't sure she liked.

The only man she wanted to dance with hadn't even approached her. He'd followed her every move but hadn't made one of his own. Glen must've been reading her thoughts, though, because as soon as the music ended, he squeezed through the maze of people and stopped directly in front of her.

"The next dance is mine," he announced, his grim eyes challenging her to contradict him.

She stared at him, astonished. This was a side of her friend she'd never seen. Demanding, intense. Generally he took everything in his stride, live and let live, that sort of thing. But this... Ellie didn't know what to think.

"You've danced with Richard three times now. It's my turn."

"You're counting?"

"Yes," he snapped. He grasped her about the waist, dragged her close and clenched her hands as if expecting Pete to break into the "Beer Barrel Polka."

"Isn't this dance mine?" Richard asked with a look of sardonic surprise.

"She's dancing with me," Glen responded before she had a chance to answer.

"Ellie?" Richard turned to her with lifted brows.

Glen's arms tightened around her defiantly.

"It's all right,' she assured the other man. "I'll dance with Glen." She waited until Richard had left the dance floor, then burst out, "What's gotten into you?" She had to raise her chin to look him in the eye.

"Plenty," he responded gruffly.

The music started again and Glen whirled her to the opposite side of the room and as far away as possible from Richard. The dance number was a mournful ballad about love gone wrong. Ellie found it a fitting choice. Couples flocked onto the dance floor, their arms around each other like clinging blackberry vines.

Glen didn't say anything, but he held her close, arms tight, jaw tense. But gradually he relaxed and so did she. They'd just found their rhythm when Richard approached and tapped Glen on the shoulder.

"My turn," he said with the smug certainty of a man who knew he'd eventually get what he wanted.

Ellie saw Glen's eyes flare in annoyance before he slowly released her. With his high sense of drama Richard grabbed her about the waist and dipped her backward until Ellie gasped, thinking her feet were about to go out from under her. Then Richard pulled her upright and danced her to the other side of the room, away from Glen.

Just when she'd adjusted her steps comfortably to Richard's, Glen was back. Without a word he tapped Richard on the shoulder. Richard gave Glen a flinty-eyed glare, then unwillingly released her.

Glen gathered her back in his arms, but they hadn't taken more than a couple of steps before Richard interrupted a second time. The two men scowled at each other.

"This is ridiculous!" Ellie cried. "What's the matter with you, Glen?"

"Me?" he exploded.

"You heard the lady," Richard said with a mocking smile that suggested Glen was making a nuisance of himself.

"You're no better," she snapped, hands aggressively on her hips.

The music faded and the couples closest to them stopped dancing to stare at the unfolding scene. Ellie had never been so embarrassed in her life. Before another minute had passed, Frank Hennessey was standing between the two men. Although he wasn't at the dance in his capacity as sheriff, he was the law in town and no one questioned his right to intervene. Dovie Boyd, who was with him, cast Ellie a sympathetic look.

"Is there a problem here, boys?" Frank asked, placing emphasis on the last word. It was a not-so-subtle reminder that this sort of skirmish was generally reserved for adolescents.

"Nothing Richard and I can't settle *outside*," Glen said.

"Glen!" Ellie couldn't believe her ears.

"That's fine with me," Richard answered quickly, raising his fists.

"Just one minute." Frank put a hand on each man's shoulder. "No one's going outside. If there's anything to settle, we'll do it right here and now." He nodded at Glen. "What's the problem?"

"I'd like to finish the dance with Ellie without Richard cutting in."

"Hey, it's a free country," Richard said, his tone cocky.

"Richard and I can settle this between us, man to man." Glen flexed his hands a number of times, letting Richard know he welcomed the opportunity to shove a fist down his throat.

"Neither of you is leaving this hall," Frank stated in a friendly but unmistakably firm tone. "At least not in your present frame of mine."

"I asked Ellie to dance first," Richard insisted.

"The hell you did!" Glen shouted.

"Ellie?" Frank turned his attention to her. "Which one of them yahoos you want to dance with?"

She glanced from one man to the other. Richard wore a smug contemptuous look and Glen's dark brooding expression didn't make her feel much better. It was as if he thought he had squatter's rights or something.

"Neither one," she announced coolly.

Glen's mouth sagged open. "Fine," he muttered.

"But, sweetheart..." Richard objected.

Unwilling to listen to either one of them, Ellie turned abruptly and muttered to Dovie and Frank, "I'm going to get a glass of punch." Glen and Richard were insufferable fools, she told herself, both of them plagued with oversize egos. She refused to allow them to make an idiot out of her, too.

Every eye in the room was focused on Ellie as she marched off the dance floor. She could feel the heat building in her face; she could hear the curious whispers all over the room.

Savannah and Caroline met her at the edge of the dance floor and gathered close around her. "Are you all right?" Savannah asked.

Ellie didn't know how to answer. Glen and Richard had made spectacles of themselves and a laughingstock of her. "I'm so furious I could scream."

Savannah nodded. "I know exactly what you mean. Sit down and I'll get you a glass of punch. It'll calm your nerves."

In her present mood it would take a whole lot more than a cold drink to calm her. Thankfully the music had started again, and as people resumed dancing, they seemed to have forgotten the incident. To Ellie's annoyance, Savannah wasn't the one who returned with the punch; Glen brought it to her, instead. She glared up at him before accepting the glass.

He stood beside her for a couple of moments, then wordlessly claimed the empty chair next to hers.

Ellie crossed her legs and turned slightly, granting him a partial view of her back.

"You might have let me know," he said after several tense minutes.

"Know what?"

"That you'd accepted Richard's invitation to the dance."

"Oh, that's rich." She twisted around to face him, struggling to keep her voice under control. "You make a point of asking if I was going to be at the dance and I thought— I *assumed*... I spent a fortune on the dress, and the next thing I hear, you invited Nell."

"You bought that dress for me?" His face brightened

and the beginnings of a smile edged up the corners of his mouth.

"You'd look pretty silly in a dress, Glen Patterson. No, I bought it for me."

He grinned roguishly at that, but his amusement faded when it became clear that Ellie was about to end the conversation.

"You'll note I'm not here with Nell," he said softly.

"Nell came with Grady, then."

"Grady asked her, too?" Glen's mouth snapped shut and he leaned hard against the back of the chair. He focused his attention on the dance floor. "I'd never have invited her if you hadn't agreed to go with Richard. I thought you and I were going to meet here."

"That's what I thought, too."

"But you said yes to Richard, anyway."

Ellie bristled. "I didn't until I'd heard you'd asked Nell."

Glen's face went blank, then his eyes narrowed suspiciously. "Why, that slimy..." he muttered. "Richard told me—" Glen stopped abruptly as if he'd already said more than he intended.

"Told you what?" Ellie pressed.

"Nothing. It doesn't matter," he muttered.

"There's no need to get short-tempered with me." Ellie crossed her arms and glared straight ahead.

Beside her, Glen crossed his arms, too, and scowled darkly at the other side of the room.

IT WAS NOW OR NEVER, Caroline decided. Pete Hadley had just announced that the next dance was ladies' choice. Heart pounding, Caroline slowly approached Grady. He sat next to Cal Patterson, and they were deeply involved in conversation. Her guess was that it had something to do with Glen and Ellie. The pair were the subject of a great deal of comment tonight. Little wonder, considering the scene they'd created earlier. Both of them now sat at the end of a row of seats, arms crossed and looking about as miserable as any two people could get.

About as miserable as *she'd* been the past few days— since her most recent encounter with Grady.

Couples were already heading toward the dance floor, and if she waited any longer, she'd miss the opportunity entirely. Savannah, on Laredo's arm, cast her an encouraging smile and nodded in Grady's direction. Savannah had actually been the one to persuade her to clear the air with Grady.

Grady and Cal's conversation halted as she reached them. Grady looked up at her as if he couldn't imagine why she was standing in front of him, blocking his view.

"Would you care to dance?" she asked, gesturing weakly toward the couples already circling the polished floor. Her pulse increased by fifty beats a minute, and she was sure he was going to humiliate her by refusing.

Grady frowned.

"It's ladies' choice," she elaborated, her voice growing small.

Grady glanced to either side. "You're asking *me?*"

"No," she snapped, her anger saving her. "I thought I'd start at the front of the row and work my way down. If you refuse, I'll ask Cal next. Come on, Grady, it shouldn't be such a difficult decision."

It seemed for a moment as if he was about to decline, then, to her enormous relief, he got to his feet. "I'm not much good at this," he muttered.

He walked stiffly at her side to the dance floor. Then he put his arm around her waist, but maintained a space between them as if he feared she carried something contagious.

"I don't generally bite," she said, amused more than insulted.

"Promise?" he asked, and drew her somewhat closer.

The music was soft and mellow, and they shuffled their feet a bit, not really dancing, which was fine with Caroline. Her skill was limited, too. She looked out over the dance floor and recognized quite a few couples. Savannah and Laredo were lost in each other's arms. How she envied the happiness her friend had found. Caroline's heart ached with a sudden loneliness for that kind of love and contentment.

"Why'd you ask me to dance?" Grady asked gruffly.

"I figured I'd have to," she said. "The last time we spoke, you said *I'd* have to ask *you*."

She felt some of the stiffness leave his body. "In other words the ball's in my court now."

Caroline grinned. "Something like that."

Grady's hold on her tightened and he gave a deep sigh as he eased her closer. For several moments, neither one spoke.

Caroline knew she'd have to bring up the subject of their last argument. This was her opportunity to mend fences with Grady, and she didn't want to waste it. "I felt bad after our conversation the other day."

"I did, too," he said. "I'm a bit of a hothead."

"And I'm too impatient."

They didn't seem to have much more to say after that, and before long the dance was over.

"I didn't step on your toes, did I?" he said as they walked off the floor.

"I seem to have survived."

He grinned, and she smiled back. Caroline held her breath, hoping maybe now he'd ask her to dance. He didn't.

"Thanks," he said when they returned to the sitting area.

"You're welcome." Caroline turned away, swallowing her disappointment.

GLEN COULDN'T SIT STILL. He'd been home from the dance for an hour and hadn't stayed in any one position for longer than five minutes. He sat down in front of the television, then bolted upright and stalked to the kitchen, thinking feverishly.

He brewed himself a cup of instant coffee and carried it into the living room. Cal was watching the late-night newscast and glanced curiously in his direction.

Glen sat back down, but was squirming a few minutes later.

"What in tarnation is the matter with you?" Cal demanded when Glen bounded out of the recliner for the sixth time in as many minutes.

"Nothing's wrong," Glen lied.

"You're thinking about Ellie again, aren't you?"

He was, but Glen had no intention of admitting it. "What makes you say that?"

Cal gave a bark of laughter. "Because, little brother, you've got it written all over you."

"Got what?"

"You've fallen for Ellie."

Glen opened his mouth to deny it, but changed his mind. After the spectacle he'd made of himself in front of the entire community, he'd look like an even bigger fool claiming otherwise. He did have feelings for Ellie, but he hadn't decided what they were. He was protective of her, like a brother, but his reactions to Richard and his behavior that evening had proved it was more than that. He wasn't sure anymore what he felt.

"Richard drove her home," he muttered, stating for the first time what had been on his mind since leaving the dance.

"You don't trust him to be a gentleman?"

"Damn right, I don't." The more Glen thought about Richard alone with Ellie, the more agitated he got. It would be just like that scumbag to try something with her. Ellie knew how to handle herself, but she was vulnerable, and Richard was just the kind of man who'd try to take advantage of that.

"I'm driving into town," he announced. He wanted to reassure himself that Richard had gone—and he wanted to talk to Ellie.

"Now?" Cal glanced at his watch. "It's nearly midnight."

"I don't care what time it is." Decision made, Glen reached for his jacket and hurried to the door. He should have followed Ellie home, that was what he should've done, but they'd barely spoken after their big scene.

"You might phone her first," Cal suggested.

Glen paused and considered his brother's idea, then shook his head. "I have things to say, and that's best done face-to-face."

"What are you going to say to her this time of night?" Cal wanted to know.

"I'm not sure yet," Glen admitted, letting the screen door bang shut. He hadn't worked anything out; maybe the moment would bring some inspiration.

The drive into town was accomplished in record time. He parked on her street, drew a couple of shaky breaths and headed for her house. He rang the bell, and when she didn't immediately appear, he pounded on the door.

The porch light went on and then he heard Ellie moving about on the other side. "Who's there?"

"Glen!" he shouted loud enough to wake half the neighborhood. "Open up, Ellie. I need to talk to you."

"It's the middle of the night," she protested, but he heard the lock turn.

She was wearing a flannel robe cinched at the waist. Her hair was mussed and he could see he'd roused her from bed. She didn't invite him inside, which was just as well.

"I'm warning you," she muttered. "This had better be important."

"It is." Then to his acute embarrassment, his mind went blank. Not only that, he couldn't keep his eyes off her. Even without makeup, her hair flattened on one side, she was beautiful. It astonished him that he'd spent all that time with her week after week, year after year, and never really seen her.

"Would you kindly stop staring at me!"

Glen hadn't realized he was. "Is Richard with you?" he asked, and knew immediately that this was the worst possible thing he could have said.

In response Ellie slammed the door in his face.

Glen clutched the frame, knocked his forehead against the door and gritted his teeth. Hoping she'd give him the opportunity to redeem himself, he pressed the doorbell again.

"Ellie, I'm sorry, I didn't mean that," he shouted, praying she could hear him.

His apology was met with silence. Then finally, "Go away."

"I can't," he said, utterly miserable.

The porch light went out. Feeling completely dejected and the biggest fool who'd ever roamed the earth, he sat on the top step. He propped his elbows on his knees and dangled his hands between his legs, lacking even the energy to get up and walk to his truck.

He must have sat there a good ten minutes before he heard the door open softly behind him. If he hadn't been so thoroughly depressed, he would have leaped to his feet and begged Ellie to forgive him. But in his current frame of mind, he was convinced she'd phoned Sheriff Hennessey. He wouldn't have blamed her.

To his surprise she sat down next to him.

"I'm sorry, Ellie," he whispered, still not looking at her. "I can't believe I asked you something so stupid."

"I can't believe you did, either."

"I kept thinking about him driving you home, and I don't know, something crazy came over me." Even knowing he'd probably infuriate her further, Glen asked, "Did he kiss you?"

She groaned and, leaning forward, buried her face in her hands.

"Is that a yes or a no?"

"It means it's none of your business."

So Richard *had* kissed her. Glen would bet just about anything on that. It was obvious; otherwise she'd have been quick to deny it. His heart sank. At one time it wouldn't have bothered him, but now it did. A hell of a lot.

"What's happened to us?" she asked. "We used to be such good friends."

"We were," he agreed. "Good friends."

"And then you kissed me."

Talk about mistakes—but Glen really couldn't make himself regret that kiss. He'd relived it for days, remembering how it felt to hold Ellie in his arms, taste her lips, touch her hair. How it felt to be so *close*.

"Damn me if you want, but I'd give anything to kiss you right now," he whispered.

He was aware of her scrutiny and half turned to meet her gaze. "Because you think Richard kissed me earlier?" she asked.

"No," he said softly. "Because I need to." He reached for her, and his heart swelled with joy when she met his lips with an eagerness that matched his own. This was what he'd wanted, what he'd needed all along. Ellie in his arms. Ellie at his side.

''This is what I want, too,'' she whispered, her lips moving over his.

Glen kissed her again. For the first time that evening—that entire week—he was at peace.

Chapter Seven

Ellie slipped into the pew Sunday morning five minutes after the service had started. Organ music surged through the church as she took the last seat, reached for the hymnal and joined the congregation in song. At first she suspected the attention she'd generated was due to her tardiness. It wasn't that she'd overslept. Far from it. The night had been her most restless since before her father's death.

She'd tossed and turned and fretted, and when sleep finally claimed her, it was fitful. She blamed Glen for that—and for a whole lot more. It was because of him she was late, but at the moment she'd have been willing to blame him for global warming.

Even after the song had ended and Pastor Wade McMillen started his sermon, Ellie felt the scrutiny of friends and neighbors. That, too, could be directly attributed to Glen. The man had single-handedly made her the object of speculation and gossip. Wringing his neck would be too good for him. First he'd embarrassed her in front of the entire town by making a spectacle of himself fighting over her. If that wasn't enough, he'd woken her out of a dead sleep, insulted her—then kissed her senseless. Ellie couldn't recall a time anyone had confused her more.

Not that she was Richard's champion. No way! He'd intentionally provoked Glen, leading him to believe the two of them were involved when it simply wasn't true. Besides, Richard was selfish and untrustworthy, and Glen was... Glen. Her friend.

Naturally Glen had skipped church. Richard, too. No doubt the effort of carting around their massive egos had worn them out, she thought irritably. It might have helped had they shown up to divide the attention now directed solely at her.

By concentrating on Wade's sermon, she managed to pretend she didn't notice her newfound celebrity status. At the end of the service following the benediction, she hoped to slip away unnoticed; it soon became apparent that this wasn't going to happen. The organ music filled the church as the congregation started to flow outside and Ellie was surrounded.

"I saw everything," Louise Powell purred, sidling up to Ellie as though they were long-standing friends. "It isn't every woman who has two men virtually at each other's throats."

"I think you misunderstood what happened," Ellie said desperately.

"I've known Glen Patterson all my life," Ruth Bishop was saying behind Louise, "and when he wants something, he gets it."

"I wouldn't underestimate Richard Weston," Louise said. "He's a man of the world. Ellie could do worse."

Ellie hated it when people spoke as if they knew more about her life than she did.

"Stay close to me," Edwina Moorhouse whispered, suddenly slipping next to Ellie and taking her arm. "Lily," she instructed her younger sister, "go on the other side." Again for Ellie's ears only, she added, "Just keep walking. We'll have you out of here in no time."

Ellie found herself grateful for the Moorhouse sister's protection. Especially from Louise Powell, the town gossip, a woman who enjoyed meddling in the affairs of others, often under the guise of concern.

"Ladies, ladies," Louise said in a sharp voice, tagging behind Ellie and the Moorhouse sisters. "*I* was chatting with Ellie."

"You aren't any longer," Edwina declared, stepping in front of Ellie.

If it hadn't been so ridiculous, and if she hadn't felt so tired and worn-out, Ellie would have laughed. Each sister positioned herself in a way that told Louise she'd have a fight on her hands before they'd willingly abandon Ellie. The two unlikely guardians were dressed in their Sunday best, with crisp white gloves and pillbox hats.

"All I wanted to do—"

"We know very well what you were doing, Louise," Edwina said in a voice that reminded Ellie of her school-days.

"Louise," Lily said, not unkindly, "do you remember in sixth grade when Larry Marino…"

Louise's face turned beet red. "I remember," she whispered.

"It would be embarrassing if news of you and Larry somehow got around town, wouldn't it?"

"That was nearly forty years ago!" Louise protested.

"And just as scandalous today as it was back then," Lily said primly. "Now, as Edwina was saying, Ellie's with *us*."

"Oh, all right." The other woman flounced off with her rumpled dignity and returned to where her husband stood impatiently waiting.

"Lily!" Edwina gasped. "What happened between Louise and Larry in the sixth grade?"

Lily covered her mouth with her hand. "God's honest truth, sister, I don't know."

"Sister, you amaze me."

"You!" Ellie giggled. She could certainly have dealt with a busybody like Louise Powell on her own, but this was much more fun.

Edwina waited until Louise was out of earshot, then she turned around and regarded Ellie with deep affection. "Are you all right, Ellie?"

"Of course."

"I'd like to box a few ears," Lily said. "We didn't teach our students to stare, did we, sister?"

"Positively not."

"I hope you're willing to forgive everyone's curiosity?"

"It's only natural, I suppose," Ellie said agreeably. "Especially in light of what happened at the dance."

"Yes, we did hear about that." Lily patted Ellie's hand. "I realize you didn't ask Edwina's or my advice, but I feel compelled to offer you a few words of wisdom."

"Since your mother isn't here," Edwina inserted.

"Please do." Ellie had always loved the Moorhouse sisters and wouldn't even consider turning down anything they offered.

"We may never have married, but Edwina and I do know a thing or two about love."

"I'm sure that's true."

Edwina caught Ellie's hand in her own. "Follow your heart, child."

"Yes, indeed, follow your heart," Lily echoed.

"I will," Ellie promised, and she would, just as soon as her heart had sorted everything out.

Still thinking about their advice, Ellie drove home, stopping first at the grocery store to pick up a few essentials. When she turned onto her street, she noticed the pickup outside her house. She groaned when she found Richard sitting on her porch, waiting for her return.

He was the last person she wanted to see. Not that she was ready to see Glen anytime soon, either. She refused to think about the kisses they'd shared or the reasons he'd come by her house after the disastrous dance. Her fear was that he saw Richard and himself as rivals for her. And that this had influenced his actions and his declarations.

What he didn't know was that Richard hadn't kissed her. Not for lack of trying, mind you, but because she was in no mood for him or his games.

Realizing she had no escape, Ellie pulled into her driveway and climbed out of the car. Richard glanced up, apparently surprised to see her loaded down with groceries.

"Ellie," he said, smiling brightly. He leaped to his feet and raced down the steps to take the bags out of her arms. "You should have said something," he chastised as if he'd waited all day for the honor of carrying her groceries.

Ellie tried to refuse his help, but he'd have none of it. "Hey, it's the least I can do." It also gave him the perfect excuse to follow her into the house, Ellie noted despondently.

He set the bags on the kitchen counter and immediately started unpacking them. "Look at this," he said as if finding a dozen eggs was akin to discovering gold. "I swear I was thinking just five minutes ago how much I'd enjoy a mushroom-and-Swiss-cheese omelet." Gesturing like a magician, he pulled a paper sack of mushrooms free of the bag, along with a slab of Swiss cheese. "It's fate," he said, his eyes twinkling.

"Richard, I don't think—"

"I'll cook," he said. He clasped her shoulders and backed her into a kitchen chair. "Sit down and make yourself at home."

"I am home," she interrupted, amused despite herself at his audacity.

He stopped a moment and smiled, then said, "So you are."

She started to stand, but he wouldn't allow it.

"I'm cooking," he said cheerfully, pushing her into the chair again.

"Richard—"

"I won't take no for an answer." He opened the cupboard door and took out a small bowl. Before Ellie could stop him, he was whirling about her kitchen as if he'd been cooking there his entire life.

To his credit he seemed to know what he was doing.

"You look especially lovely this morning," he said, pouring the eggs into the skillet.

"Yeah, yeah." Ellie was in no mood for empty flattery. "I've heard that before."

"Only because it's true." He whistled something jaunty as he edged a spatula under the omelet.

The doorbell rang and with a wave of his hand Richard motioned for her to answer it.

Ellie was too concerned with how to expel Richard from her home to be affronted by his peremptory manner—or to worry about who'd come calling unannounced. Hindsight being what it was, she wished later she'd given the matter some thought before she opened the door.

Glen Patterson stood on the other side.

Ellie's mouth fell open. She hadn't expected to see him. "Glen!"

"Who is it, sweetheart?" Richard asked, stepping out of the kitchen, a dish towel tucked at his waist. He carried the frying pan and spatula in his hands and didn't miss a beat when he saw Glen.

"Howdy, neighbor," he called. "I'm stirring up a little brunch here. You're welcome to join us if you want."

Glen's eyes hardened as he looked at Ellie. She tried to tell him without words that it wasn't how it seemed; that she hadn't *asked* Richard to join her, he'd come uninvited. But Glen had already formed his own opinion, and nothing she did now was likely to change it.

"I'll be back another time," he muttered.

"Stay," Richard urged like a gracious host. "Cooking is one of my talents. Ask Ellie."

It was all she could manage not to wheel around and kick Richard in the shin.

THREE DAYS HAD PASSED since Glen had stumbled on Richard cooking Ellie's breakfast. Three miserable days. He still couldn't think about it and not get mad.

He hadn't seen Ellie, hadn't talked to her in those three days. Generally he dropped in the feed store for supplies on Tuesday afternoons. Almost always they'd spend a few minutes together, joking, teasing, laughing. There'd been damn little of that lately. He didn't drive into town on Tuesday, and he wasn't eager to make the trip on Wednesday, either. It would do Ellie good to miss his company, not that he'd received any indication that she had.

Ellie preyed on his mind, making him next to useless around the ranch. Disgusted, Cal sent him out to check fence lines. If that was meant to distract him, it hadn't worked. Grandpa Patterson used to say: never approach a bull from the front, a horse from the rear or a fool from any direction. Well, Glen couldn't help feeling like a fool, and his mind seemed to be spinning in *every* direction.

His thinking was clouded with thoughts of Ellie as he trotted back toward the ranch. When he wasn't thinking about her, he was brooding about Richard Weston. Glen feared Richard was using the time he stayed away from Ellie to further his own cause.

If that was true, then so be it. If Ellie wanted Richard, fine, she was welcome to him but he'd figured she had more sense.

A man had his pride, too. Glen had kissed Ellie on two occasions now, and if he could recognize that they had something pretty special, why couldn't she? Okay, so they hadn't talked about their feelings, but Glen had been hoping to do that on Sunday. Only he couldn't, because Richard was there, playing Julia Child.

The way he saw it, Ellie owed him an apology. She'd misled him, kissing him like she had, then cozying up to Richard. He'd never have taken Ellie for the type of woman who'd play one man against another, but he'd seen the evidence with his own eyes.

Cal was waiting for him when he led Moonshine into the barn.

"Are you picking up supplies this week or not?" Cal demanded.

"I'll get them," Glen replied without enthusiasm.

"If it's a problem, I'll drive into town myself."

"It's no problem," Glen said. Damn it, he couldn't stay away a minute longer, and he knew it.

By the time Glen cleaned up and drove into town, his throat was parched. More to fortify his courage than to cure his thirst, he decided to stop at Billy D's for a cold beer.

Billy D himself was behind the bar when Glen sauntered in. The ranchers tended to congregate here when they came to town, and there was usually someone he knew. Billy was the friendly sort and something of an institution in Promise. He baked a decent pizza, and his fried chicken was as good as any colonel's; but few people came to Billy D's for the food. It was the one place in town, other than the bowlng alley and the feed store, where ranchers could shoot the breeze and unwind. And at Billy's they could do it over a beer.

"Well if it ain't Glen Patterson himself," Billy called out when Glen walked in.

A couple of ranchers lounging against the bar raised their hands in greeting.

Glen tipped his Stetson a little farther back on his head.

"You want a cold one?" Billy asked.

"Sounds good." Glen stepped up to the bar and set some money down on the counter.

With practiced ease Billy slid the thick mug down the polished bar and Glen grabbed it before it flew past.

"Keep your money. It's on the house," Billy said, smiling broadly.

Glen arched his brows and lifted the mug to his lips. Nothing tasted better than a cold beer on a hot day, especially when it was free. It slid down the back of his throat, easing away the taste of several hours of eating dust.

"Any reason you're giving away beer this afternoon?" he asked when he'd downed half the mug.

"Only to you," Billy informed him.

"What's so special about me?"

Billy gave him a look that suggested he open his eyes. "I figure you're gonna set Richard Weston on his ear. In fact, I'm waitin' to see it."

Glen frowned. "I don't have any fight with Weston." Ellie would probably love it if he acted like an idiot—yet again—but he was finished with that game. Those two were welcome to each other. Glen had decided to wash his hands of the whole thing. If Ellie wanted to marry Richard, then he wasn't going to stand in her way.

"You don't care?" Billy looked as if he wanted his beer back. "Richard's been by, and to hear him talk, he's done everything but put an engagement ring on Ellie's finger. You aren't going to let that happen, are you?"

"What am I supposed to do about it?" Glen asked, hardening his heart in order to avoid showing his feelings.

Billy frowned. He braced both hands on the bar and leaned forward as though to get a better look at Glen. "You're serious about this?"

"Damn right, I'm serious."

"That's not the impression I got Saturday night. The three of you are the hot topic of conversation this week, dancing that Texas two-step of yours. Some folks've started placing bets on which of you is gonna marry Ellie.''

''As far as I'm concerned Richard can have her.'' It was a bold-faced lie, but Glen considered it damage control. For his ego *and* his reputation.

''Personally I think you're the better man,'' Lyle Whitehouse said. His back was to the bar and he'd rested his elbows behind him. Lyle worked at a ranch closer to Brewster than to Promise, but he'd worn out his welcome at more than a few places. He had a reputation as a hothead, although he hadn't started any fights at Billy D's. Yet.

Jimmy Morris stood beside him, his stomach pressed to the bar and one boot on the brass foot rail. ''When you're talkin' marriage, it isn't a matter of bein' better,'' he said ponderously. ''Ladies choose who they choose.''

''True enough,'' Lyle agreed. ''But it doesn't hurt to try a bit of persuasion...'' He winked. ''You know what I mean.''

''Richard seems to think he's got an edge on you,'' Billy informed Glen, ''and no one likes a man who's too confident.''

''Even if he does buy the drinks,'' Jimmy added.

''Richard's celebrating already?'' Glen asked, wondering if Richard knew something no one else did. Maybe he'd already asked Ellie and maybe she'd given him an encouraging response. The thought twisted his gut. To this point he'd trusted Ellie's judgment. More or less. He was miserable and uncertain about her and Richard, but he'd always supposed that in the end Ellie would turn to him. Because of their friendship and everything they had in common...and their kisses.

Those kisses in the wee hours of Saturday night had been wonderful, the best of his life. He found it hard to believe they'd meant so little to her.

''Weston's so sure of himself he's taking odds.''

"Making himself the favorite," Billy said, his mouth thinning with disapproval.

"Naturally," Jimmy muttered, and took a swallow of beer.

"We were kinda hopin' you'd set him down a peg or two," Lyle said in a tone that suggested more than one rancher had pinned his hopes on Glen.

Glen didn't know what it was about Richard Weston. He'd never met anyone so likable, yet so universally disliked. He could be charming, witty and fun, and at the same time he was the biggest jackass in the state of Texas.

"What do you think?" Billy pressed.

"You're not gonna take this sittin' down, are you?" Lyle asked.

"You gotta do something," Jimmy added. "We got money on you!"

All three men looked to Glen. Unfortunately he didn't know *what* the hell to do.

ONE OF THE MOST DIFFICULT things Richard Weston had ever done was return to Promise—broke, his tail between his legs, seeking a handout from his family. Once he was home again, he figured he'd die of sheer boredom inside a month. Promise was about as Hicktown, U.S.A., as it could get. He stared at the walls of his old bedroom and sighed. Never in a million years did he guess he'd end up back here.

What intrigued him was how gullible folks in Promise were. Everyone—well, except for the sheriff and he couldn't *prove* anything—accepted his lies without pause or question. In fact, he'd gotten a little careless, but it didn't seem to matter. He'd certainly been right in assuming that he'd be safe here, at the ranch—safe from his troubles back east.

The boredom, though. He sighed. And the cows...

It'd taken him the better part of six years to get the stench of cattle from his skin. He'd never understood the attraction of following a bunch of pathetic-looking beasts from pasture to pasture. As far as he was concerned, cattle were headaches on the hoof. Yet his father and his brother had always acted as though there was nothing more wonderful in life than ranching. But it sure wasn't for him; never had been, never would be. The mere thought of sitting in a saddle all day made him want to puke, although God knew Grady had done his best to get him to do some work around the place. Thus far, he'd managed to avoid doing anything of consequence. He'd volunteered to run errands, which gave him free use of the pickup—something that had come in handy for other reasons. The tradespeople around Promise trusted him, assumed he was taking care of ranch business. And he was. But he was seeing to his own needs, as well.

To his surprise he'd discovered some pleasant distractions in Promise. Ellie Frasier, for one. She was a sweet thing, pretty, too, if a guy didn't mind small breasts and skinny legs. Personally he preferred a more voluptuous woman, but Ellie came with certain monetary compensations. A prosperous business, plus a healthy inheritance from her daddy, who'd doted on his only child.

It wouldn't hurt him any to get his hands on old-man Frasier's money. He could use it. He was in trouble, but all it took was money in the right places and his problem would vanish.

For now he was safe enough in Promise. No one knew about his family, and even if they managed to track him to Texas, they'd never find his hiding place.

He had Savannah to thank for that. He'd always been lucky—at least until his present difficulties. But then, everything had a way of working out. This latest episode was a good example.

No, he decided, lying on top of his quilt, hands folded behind his head, there could be worse things in this world than marrying Ellie Frasier. He'd ask her soon, and if she was opposed to selling the business, then he'd take it over. He could do well with it, too—aside from the fact that it would provide collateral for raising quick cash.

Actually Richard liked the idea of becoming a local businessman. He could remember one of his teachers, Lily Moorhouse, telling him he should be a politician. The old biddy just could be right. In a year or two he might even consider running for mayor. Promise could use his kind of leadership. This hayseed town needed someone to bring it into the twenty-first century.

The town had real possibilities, if he could convince people to listen to his ideas. For starters they needed to close down the bowling alley; in his view it gave the place a white-trash image. He'd buy up land outside town and get some investors to build a shopping complex. If not that, he'd bet he could get one of the big discount stores interested in the area. It was time the local shop owners found out about competitive pricing.

Everything hinged on Ellie. They'd kissed a couple of times, and although she didn't exactly set him ablaze, she wasn't bad. He knew she was sweet on Glen Patterson. That might be cause for concern if Patterson wasn't so intent on putting his foot in his mouth, which he seemed to do with increasing regularity. Fortunately for Richard.

Poor guy was out of his league with women, unlike Richard who had the whole mating ritual down to an art. The way he figured it, Ellie would agree to marry him before the end of the month. Maybe sooner. When he turned on the charm, there wasn't a female within six states who could refuse him. Little Ellie Frasier didn't have a snowball's chance in hell.

And over at Billy D's Richard stood to pick up a few

extra bucks betting on his own chances in the Texas two-step.

Altogether a sweet deal.

FOR MOST OF HIS ADULT life Glen had been confident and self-assured. He'd taken over the family ranch with his brother, worked hard, kept his nose clean. Romantic involvements had been light and ultimately insignificant, causing no pain when they ended. Until now there'd been little to disrupt his calm existence.

Any problems he either solved himself or sought advice from Cal. This was the first time since he was thirteen years old that he felt the need to speak to his father about girls. Women. What his grandfather used to call "personal matters."

His parents had moved into town a few years ago. His father had suffered a heart attack, and although the doctors had said he was good as new following his bypass surgery, his mother wasn't taking any chances. For years they'd talked about moving into Promise one day. His father had insisted he wasn't ready to retire, so they'd bought the Howe Mansion, which wasn't really a mansion, just the largest house in town. Before another year was up it'd been renovated and turned into a bed-and-breakfast.

Glen had had his doubts about this venture. Cal, too. But their parents had proved them both wrong. The bed-and-breakfast was thriving, and so were Phil and Mary Patterson.

His mother complained that she didn't see near enough of her sons. That being the case, she certainly looked surprised to see Glen when he walked into her kitchen.

"Hi, Mom," he said, slipping up behind her and kissing her cheek.

Mary Patterson hugged him as though it'd been a week

of Sundays since his last visit. "Taste this," she said, sticking a spoon in his face.

"What is it?" Glen asked, jerking his head back. He preferred not to be part of a culinary experiment.

"Chili. I'm practicing for the cook-off."

"Mom, that's not for months yet."

"I know. This is a new recipe I've been playing around with. What do you think?"

Despite his better judgment, Glen tried the chili and tried to hide his response. It tasted...well, not like food. Not like something you'd seriously consider eating.

"It needs work, right?" she asked, studying him.

He nodded. For her guests his mother generally stayed with plain basic food. Good thing. "This recipe needs a rethink, Mom."

She sighed and tossed the spoon into the sink. "I was afraid of that."

"Where's Dad?" Glen asked, hoping to make the inquiry sound casual.

"Upstairs. The sink in the bathroom's plugged again." Her gaze didn't waver from his. "Something on your mind?"

He nodded. He could never hide anything from his mother.

"Does it involve Ellie Frasier?"

"Yeah."

She grinned and pointed toward the stairway off the kitchen. "Talk to your father, but if you want advice about how to romance her, talk to me. Your father doesn't know a damn thing about romance."

Hiding a smile, Glen headed for the stairs. Just as his mother had said, he found his dad lying on the tile floor staring up at the sink, wrench in hand.

"Hi, Dad."

"I thought I heard you downstairs talking to your

mother." Phil Patterson slid out from beneath the sink and reached for a rag to dry his hands. "And to think she was worried about me working too hard on the ranch. If anything's going to kill me, it'll be this sink."

Glen sat down on the edge of the tub.

"Did you have something you wanted to ask me, son?"

Leaning forward, Glen removed his Stetson, slowly turning it in his hands. "How many years have you and Mom been married?"

"Well, your brother's thirty-six, so this year we had our thirty-seventh anniversary. Thirty-seven years! Damn, it doesn't seem that long. Hell if I can figure out when I got old."

"You're not."

Phil smiled. "That's my boy. Buttering me up, are you? So what do you need?"

"Just some advice."

"Be glad to help if I can." With an exaggerated groan, he stood up, lowered the toilet seat and sat there.

Glen wasn't sure where to start. "When did you know you loved Mom?"

Phil considered the question for a moment. "When she told me I did." He chuckled and Glen joined in. "Don't laugh too hard, boy, it's the truth. We'd dated in high school some, but she was two years younger. After I graduated, I enlisted. Joined the Navy. We wrote back and forth and I saw a little of the world. Eventually your mother graduated and went away to college in Dallas. We didn't see each other for three years, but we kept in touch. I must say she wrote a lot more letters than me.

"Then one Christmas, we both happened to be home at the same time. It was a shock to see her again. We'd been friends, stayed in touch, but somehow I'd never noticed how pretty she was."

Glen nodded; his mother was still a pretty woman.

"I wasn't the only one who noticed, either," his father continued. "She got more attention than a prize heifer at the state fair. Until that Christmas I'd always thought of her as a friend. We'd dated from time to time, but it was nothing serious. That Christmas my eyes were opened."

"Did you ask her to marry you then?"

"Hell, no. I wasn't happy about other men paying attention to her, but I figured if she wanted to date someone else, I didn't have the right to stand in her way."

"You were sweet on her, though?"

"Yeah, but I didn't realize how much until we'd kissed a few times."

Now that was something Glen could understand. "Did you try to talk to her?"

Phil chuckled again. "I sure did, but all we seemed to do was argue. Nothing I said was right. I told her I thought she was pretty, and even that came out like an insult."

This story was sounding more familiar by the minute. "So what happened?"

His father grew thoughtful. "It was time to head back to the base, and I knew if I didn't try to explain myself one last time, I might not get another chance. I called her all evening, but she was out—you can imagine how *that* made me feel, especially since I couldn't very well ring her doorbell in the middle of the night." He smiled at the memory. "So I stood outside her bedroom and threw stones at the window until she woke up.

"It's not a good idea to wake your mother out of a sound sleep, even now. It took me a while to convince her to hear me out. Luckily she agreed and sat with me on the porch. By that time I was so confused I didn't know what to say."

Glen edged closer to his father, keenly interested in the details of his parents' courtship.

"I stammered and stuttered and told her how much I valued her friendship and hated the idea of returning to

Maine with this bad feeling between us. That was when she looked me full in the eye and asked if I loved her.''

His mother had always been a gutsy woman and Glen admired her for it. "What did you tell her?"

"I didn't know what to say. It was the first time I'd ever thought about it. We were friends, hung around with the same crowd, exchanged letters, that sort of thing. She wanted to know if I loved her, and for the life of me I didn't have an answer.''

It went without saying that wasn't what his mother had wanted to hear.

"When I hesitated, Mary leaped to her feet and announced I was the biggest fool who'd ever lived if I hadn't figured out how I felt about her after three years. My, was she mad.'' Shaking his head, he rubbed the side of his jaw. "Her eyes had fire in them. In all the years we've been married, I've only seen her get that riled a handful of times. She told me if I married some Yankee girl I'd regret it the rest of my life.''

He paused a moment, lost in his memories. "Then before I could stop her, she raced into the house. By the time I'd gathered my wits and followed her, she was already running up the stairs. Her father and her mother both stood on the landing, looking down at me as though they wanted to string me up from the nearest tree.''

"What'd you do?"

"What I should have done a hell of a lot sooner. I shouted up at her father for permission to marry his daughter.''

That scene filled Glen's mind. His father a young sailor, standing at the bottom of the stairs, watching the love of his life racing away. "What'd Mom do?"

"She stopped, halfway between her parents and me. I'll never forget the look of shock on her face as she turned around and stared at me.''

"She burst into tears, right?"

"No. She stood here, calm as could be and asked me when I wanted the wedding to take place. Hell if I knew, so I said that was up to her, and she suggested six months."

"I thought your anniversary was Valentine's Day."

"It is. Once we decided to get married, I wasn't willing to wait six months. By summer she was pregnant with your brother." He looked at Glen. "Why all these questions?"

"Just curious."

"You going to ask Ellie to marry you?"

"I've been thinking about it."

His father's grin widened. "Did she tell you you're in love with her yet?"

"Nope. I don't think she realizes it herself."

Phil stood and slapped him on the back. "Then start a new family tradition and tell her yourself, boy. It's about time the men in this family took the initiative."

Chapter Eight

Richard rolled out of bed and reached for his jeans. Savannah was making breakfast, and if his nose didn't deceive him, it smelled like one of his favorites. French toast.

Yawning, he grabbed a shirt on his way out the door and bounded down the stairs and into the kitchen.

"Mornin'," he said, yawning again. He glanced at the wall clock and was surprised to see it was after nine. A midmorning breakfast cooked specially for him meant his sister was planning on a little heart-to-heart. Damn.

"Morning," Savannah returned in that gentle way of hers. At times it was all he could do not to leap behind her, waving his arms and screaming at the top of his lungs. He wondered if he'd get a reaction from her even then. Somehow he doubted it.

"Grady needs you to drive into town this morning."

"No problem." Actually Richard liked running errands. They suited his purpose. Every time Grady sent him into town, he managed to pick up an item or two for himself and put it on his brother's tab without Grady's knowing a thing about it.

Savannah delivered a plate to the table where Richard sat waiting. He dug into the meal after slathering his hot toast with plenty of butter and syrup. Savannah didn't disappear, which meant the errand for Grady wasn't the only thing on her mind.

"There's been plenty of talk around town about you and Ellie," she said, clutching the back of the chair opposite his.

The tension in her fingers told him she felt awkward addressing the subject. Lord, his sister was easy to read!

"That so?" He stuffed another forkful of French toast in his mouth.

"Ellie's a real sweetheart."

He shrugged.

Savannah pulled out the chair and sat down.

Damn it, he'd asked for that. Knowing his sister was fond of the other woman, he should have talked her up, fabricated a few things, let his sister think he'd fallen in love with Ellie. He hadn't, but his interest in her was definitely high at the moment. A lot was riding on this, and if he managed to manipulate the situation to his liking, it meant staying in the community. After fixing his current problems of course. Yeah, he could see a future here. Become one of the leading lights in Promise. Turn this place around. And it all hinged on little Ellie Frasier.

"I don't want you to hurt her, Richard."

This was quite a statement from Savannah. "Hurt Ellie?" He tried to look shocked that she'd even suggest such a thing.

"Ellie's...fragile just now."

"I wouldn't dream of doing anything to hurt Ellie." He set his fork down as if to say the mere idea had robbed him of his appetite.

"Then your intentions are honorable?"

Leave it to Savannah to sound like she was living in the nineteenth century. She could've set up camp at Bitter End and fit right in.

"Of course my intentions are honorable. In fact, I intend

to ask Ellie to be my wife." Richard assumed this was what Savannah wanted to hear, but she didn't react that way he'd expected. He'd hoped that when he mentioned words like "wife" and "marriage," she'd go all feminine on him and start nattering about wedding pans.

"It's a big step for me," he added, thinking she'd be quick to praise his decision.

Savannah frowned. "I heard about this little lottery thing you've got going."

"Oh, that." He dismissed her concern with an airy gesture. Word traveled fast in small towns and he'd forgotten that.

"I don't think placing bets on...on love, on whether Ellie's going to marry you or Glen, is such a good idea."

"It was a joke," he said. What Savannah didn't understand and what he couldn't tell her was that the whole thing had gotten started when he'd had one too many beers. Naturally he'd taken a lot of ribbing about the fiasco at the dance.

The whole thing was Glen Patterson's fault. In Richard's opinion, the rancher owed him an apology. Ellie had been *his* date and Glen had been way out of line butting in at the dance.

"Joking with another person's affections—"

"I'm not joking with Ellie," Richard interrupted. "I love her, Savannah," he said, doing his best to look and sound sincere. What he really loved about Ellie Frasier was the store and her inheritance. That Ellie wasn't hard on the eyes was a bonus. Marriage wasn't such a bad idea either. He could grow accustomed to bedded bliss, not to mention regular meals. Savannah had spoiled him, preparing elaborate dinners and baking his favorite goodies, although she tended to do less of that these days.

"It isn't only Ellie I want to talk to you about."

"You mean there's more?" He tried not to sound perturbed, but really, this was getting ridiculous. He didn't need his big sister prying into his private life, nor did he appreciate this need she had to lecture him. He'd been out of the schoolroom too many years to sit still for much more of this.

His sister pursed her lips in exactly the way their mother used to. "I got a phone call from Millie about an unpaid flower bill."

"Millie?"

"You know Millie." Her tone left no room for argument.

"Oh, that Millie." He was walking a tightrope when it came to a number of charges he'd made in town during the past few months. He'd hoped to have moved on by now, but this romance with Ellie had fallen into his lap and he couldn't let the opportunity just slip through his fingers. He'd also made contingency plans—no fool he. He'd found the perfect hiding place when and if he needed it. But he couldn't leave Promise yet and perhaps not for some time. Keeping Grady and Savannah in the dark until he'd secured his future was proving to be something of a challenge.

"Millie said you owed her four hundred dollars. I realize your...check hasn't arrived yet—" she didn't meet his eyes "—but you *have* to make some kind of arrangement with Millie."

He toyed with the idea of being shocked to hear it was that much money, but thought better of it. "Well, I have just a little money left." He hoped that was vague enough so she wouldn't question it. "In fact, I was in just yesterday and made a payment," he said.

"I talked to Millie yesterday and she claimed she hadn't seen you in weeks." Savannah's eyes had never been that cool before.

"I didn't see Millie, just one of her employees."

"I didn't know Millie had anyone working for her."

Savannah pinned him with her gaze.

"Summer help, I assume," he murmured. "I've got the receipt up in my room if you want to see it." He put the right amount of indignation into his voice to make sure she understood he found her lack of trust insulting.

"If you say you made a payment, then I don't have any choice but to believe you."

Richard shoved his chair away from the table. "I'm getting the distinct impression I'm no longer welcome around here." He stopped short of reminding her he'd been born and raised in this very house, fearing that might be overkill, even with a softhearted woman like his sister.

"It isn't that."

"I've come home," he said, tilting his chin at a proud angle. "It wasn't easy to arrive on your doorstep with nothing. Now that I'm here, I've realized that I made a mistake ever leaving. Promise is my home. I've fallen in love and I want to make a new life for myself with friends and neighbors I grew up with. People I've known all my life. If you want to kick me out, then all you or Grady need to do is say the word and I'll be gone." He drew the line and dared her to cross it. Basically it was a gamble, but one he was willing to take. He'd been a gambler most of his life, after all—one who usually had an ace up his sleeve.

"I won't ask you to move," she said after a moment.

He hadn't really thought she would.

"But I'm giving you fair warning—tread lightly when it comes to Ellie."

He widened his eyes, disliking her brisk tone.

"And pay your bills. Once Grady gets wind of this, there'll be trouble. His nature isn't nearly as generous as mine."

"You haven't got a thing to worry about," Richard said, and as a conciliatory gesture, he carried his plate to the sink.

IT HAD SOUNDED so simple when Glen talked to his father nearly a week earlier. Asking Ellie to marry him had seemed the right thing to do. But Richard's interest in her had muddied an already complicated issue. From the gossip circulating around town, Weston had definitely taken advantage of the time Glen stayed away.

Fine. Great. Wonderful. If Ellie was so impressed with Richard, she could have him. At least that was what Glen told himself a dozen times a day, but no matter how often he said it, he couldn't quite make himself believe it.

"I don't know what the hell I'm going to do," he muttered. He sometimes did his thinking out loud, and talking to a horse was safer than talking to certain people. As he cleaned the gelding's hooves, Moonshine perked up his ears in apparent sympathy.

"You talking to me?" Cal shouted from the other side of the barn.

Glen didn't realize his brother was anywhere nearby. "No," he hollered, hoping to discourage further conversation.

It didn't work.

"Who you talking to, then?"

"No one!" he snapped. Glen was the first to admit he hadn't been great company lately. That was one reason he'd kept to himself as much as possible and avoided Cal.

"You still down in the mouth about Ellie?" Cal asked, sounding much closer this time.

It was on the tip of Glen's tongue to tell his brother to mind his own damn business. Lord, but he was tired of it all. Tired of being so confused by this woman he could no longer think. Tired of worrying she'd actually marry Richard. Tired of feeling miserable.

"How'd I get into this mess?" Glen asked hopelessly.

"Women specialize in wearing a man down," Cal said, peering into the stall.

''Ellie isn't Jennifer,'' Glen felt obliged to remind him. That was the problem with discussing things with Cal. His brother refused to look past the pain and embarrassment his ex-fiancée had caused him. Everything was tainted by their ruined relationship.

''I know.''

Glen lowered Moonshine's foot to the ground and slowly straightened. The small of his back ached. He pressed his hand to the area and massaged the sore muscles before he opened the stall door.

Glen watched Cal carry a bucket of oats to his own gelding. Suddenly it was all too much. He couldn't stand it any more. Damn it all, he *loved* Ellie and if she wasn't willing to come to him, then by God he'd go to her. The rush of relief he experienced was overwhelming.

''I'm asking Ellie to marry me,'' he said boldly, bracing himself for the backlash of Cal's reaction.

Cal went very still. Finally he asked, ''Is that what you want?''

''Damn straight it is.''

''Then…great.''

Glen blinked, wondering if he was hearing things. The one person he'd expected to talk him out of proposing was Cal.

''You love her?''

''Of course I do,'' Glen said. ''I wouldn't ask a woman to share my life if I didn't.''

Cal laughed and slapped Glen on the shoulder. ''So I guess congratulations are in order.''

Glen rubbed his hand across the back of his neck. He didn't feel like throwing a party just yet.

''When are you going to ask her?''

''I…I don't know yet,'' Glen confessed. He'd only decided this five seconds ago.

He glanced at his watch. If he showered quickly he could

make the drive into town and talk to Ellie before she left the shop. It seemed fitting that he ask her to marry him at the feed store, considering that most of their courtship had taken place there. At the time, however, he hadn't *realized* he'd been courting her.

"I think I'll do it tonight," he said. Feeling euphoric, he'd dashed halfway out of the barn when Cal stopped him.

"Have you got her an engagement ring?"

A ring? Damn, he hadn't thought of that. "Do I need one?"

"It doesn't hurt."

Glen could feel the panic rising up inside him. Cal must have seen it, too, because he offered Glen the ring he had in his bottom drawer.

"I've still got the one I bought for Jennifer."

"But that belongs to you."

"Go ahead and take it. It's a beautiful diamond. After Ellie agrees, then the two of you can go shopping and pick out a new one if she wants. Although this one's perfectly good."

Things were beginning to fall nicely into place. "Thanks." As Glen recalled, Cal had gone for broke buying Jennifer's diamond. Damn shame to keep it buried in a drawer. If Ellie liked that ring, he'd buy it from his brother; she need never know the ring was sightly used.

A quick shower revitalized him. He sang as he lathered up, then raised his face to the spray, laughing as the water rushed over him. When he'd finished, he shook his head like a long-haired dog fresh from a dip in the pond. Still smiling, he dressed in a clean shirt and jeans.

He felt drunk with happiness.

Glen didn't sober up until he reached town. Then and only then did the seriousness of his mission strike him. Not once had he given any thought to how he would word his proposal.

This was quite possibly the most important conversation of his life and he hadn't even rehearsed it! His father had spoken to his potential father-in-law and not the bride. But even if Ellie's father were alive, that approach didn't really work anymore. Too old-fashioned.

He thought about getting down on one knee and spilling out his heart, but immediately dismissed the idea. No one did that sort of thing these days. Much too formal. By the same token, he didn't want to make an offer of marriage sound like an invitation to go bowling, either. All he could do was hope the right approach presented itself when the moment arrived.

It was nearly closing time when he got to the store. Ellie was on the loading dock at the far end of the building, giving instructions to a delivery-truck driver as Glen parked his own truck in front of the store and turned off the engine. She damn near fell off the dock in surprise when she saw him.

That was promising, Glen thought. She must've missed him. He'd missed *her* like hell, and telling her so was probably as good a place to start as any. Having decided that much, he climbed out of the cab and walked up the steps.

"Hello, Glen," Ellie's assistant greeted.

"Hi, George."

"Good to see you," George Tucker said, then added in a low voice, "Damn good."

"Glad to hear it." Glen sat down in one of the lawn chairs by the front door near the soda machine, and waited until Ellie was free. It took almost ten minutes to supervise the unloading of a truckload of hay, but he was a patient man.

Ellie signed the necessary papers, then stood there for a moment, blinking into the sun. Her face was pink, and the hair at the back of her head was damp and clinging to her neck. It'd obviously been a long hot day.

"Do you have a few minutes?" he asked when she'd finished. "I'd like to talk to you—*privately.*" He added this last bit in case Richard was anywhere around.

"Privately," Ellie repeated. Small vertical frown lines appeared between her brows.

"There's, uh, something I'd like to discuss with you. Privately," he said again.

"Do you want a cold drink?"

It was almost like old times, he told himself. Casual, relaxed, two friends talking.

"Something cold'd hit the spot," he said, answering Ellie's question.

She retrieved change from her pocket and slipped the coins into the pop machine. She handed him one of the cold damp cans and pressed the other to her forehead, then claimed the chair beside his.

Glen opened his drink, pulling back the tab with a small hissing sound, and took a long swallow.

George appeared. "Do you need me to do anything else?" he asked.

Ellie shook her head. "You're free to go, thanks, George."

"I'll see you in the morning, then," he said, turning the Open sign to Closed on his way past.

It might have been Glen's imagination, but Ellie's assistant seemed eager to be on his way.

Ellie answered his question before he could even ask it. "It's his bowling night," she explained.

His parents were like that, Glen mused. Often, his dad didn't need to voice his thoughts for his mother to know what he was thinking. Sometimes that was true of close friends, as well. With Ellie, he could have love *and* friendship, and surely that was the best way to enter a marriage.

The late-afternoon sun blazed, but the heat didn't seem nearly as bad, now that he was sitting in the shade with

Ellie. A slight breeze stirred, cooling his skin, ruffling her hair.

"You wanted to talk to me," Ellie began.

"Yeah." Glen had hoped to make this as natural as possible.

"You haven't been in for a while," she said, staring straight ahead.

Ten days, not that Glen was keeping track or anything. Cal had taken care of the errands these past two weeks while Glen stayed close to the ranch.

"I've been busy," Glen said, deciding it probably wasn't a good idea to mention he'd been waiting to hear from her.

"So have I."

Glen could just imagine who she'd been busy with, but he didn't dare say that. Richard Weston wasn't a name he wanted to introduce into their conversation—although he did wonder how much she'd been seeing of the guy.

"I wanted to talk to you about the dance first," he said, and although he tried, he couldn't keep his voice from sounding stiff. The events of that night still rankled him.

"I don't think it's necessary, seeing how—"

"I'd like to apologize," he interrupted. If she wasn't willing to admit her part in the disaster, then he'd be man enough to seek her forgiveness for his own role.

"Oh."

"I didn't mean to make us both fodder for gossip."

"I know you didn't," she said, her voice softening perceptibly.

"You and I've been friends for quite a while now."

She nodded. "Very good friends."

Glen stuck his hand in his pocket and felt for the diamond ring. Holding on to it lent him the courage to continue. This was harder than he'd thought it would be, but too important to ruin with nerves. All he had to do was remind himself that this was Ellie, his longtime friend. In the years to come he wanted to be able to tell his children and his grandchildren about this day with the same sense of wonder and excitement he'd heard in his father's voice when he'd relayed the tale of proposing to their mother.

"Since your dad's gone, I feel a certain duty to protect you."

"A duty?" A chill edged her voice.

"Well, not a duty exactly. More of…an obligation to see that no harm befalls you." He knew he must sound stilted, kind of old-fashioned, but he couldn't seem to help it.

"What do you mean by harm?"

The hell if he knew. "Perhaps 'harm' isn't the best word, either. I want to look after you."

"I'm not a child, Glen."

"No, no, I don't mean to imply that you are." He could feel the sweat starting to break out across his forehead. Working his way up to this marriage proposal was harder than freeing a stuck calf from a mud hole. He swallowed painfully as he prepared to continue.

Ellie eyed him in consternation.

"What I'm trying to say," he started again, gulping down some air, "is— Oh, damn." He catapulted to his feet, finding it impossible to stay seated any longer. "Listen, Ellie, I'm not good at this. I'm the one responsible for embarrassing you and—"

"What the hell are you talking about?" she demanded.

Glen paced the porch, walking past the soda machine several times. "It hasn't been easy deciding what to do, I want you to know that."

"I'm not asking you to *do* anything."

"I know, but I feel responsible."

"Then I absolve you of all responsibility." She waved one arm as if holding a magic wand.

"It isn't that easy," he muttered.

"What's this all about?" she asked again.

Glen tilted his head back and expelled a long breath. This wasn't going well. He should have practiced on Cal first, at least gone over what he intended to say, sought his brother's advice.

Ellie had stood up, too.

It was now or never. Taking the plunge, he squared his shoulders and met her look head-on. "I think we should get married."

"Married!" The word exploded out of her mouth. Almost as if she'd been struck, Ellie sat back down, gripping the sides of her chair with both hands. Then...she began to laugh. A deep robust laugh.

Glen was deflated. This woman had a great deal to learn about a man's pride, he reflected sadly.

"You're serious?" she asked when her laughter had dwindled to a low chuckle.

"I have a ring," he said, pulling it out to prove his point. He held it between index finger and thumb.

Ellie's eyes widened.

Dismissing his earlier plan, he decided she should know the truth about this particular ring. "Actually I borrowed it from Cal. This is the diamond Jennifer returned when she broke the engagement."

She stared at him as if she hadn't heard a word he said.

"I couldn't very well propose without a ring," he explained. "If you don't like it, you can choose another one later, although I've got to tell you I think Cal would give us a good deal on it. But I'll leave that decision up to you."

Ellie blinked back tears and Glen relaxed. He knew once he got the word out, everything would be better.

"Why now?" she asked, her voice cracking. "What made you propose today?"

"We're friends," he said. "That's one reason. I enjoy being with you more than any woman I've ever known.

You've got a lot of excellent qualities and…'' He was running out of things to say. "Basically it's time.''

"Time?''

"To get married. I've been thinking along those lines recently—''

"Because of Richard?''

Glen had hoped to get through this conversation without any mention of the other man. He cleared his throat. "Not entirely.''

Her responding smile was slight. "At least you're honest enough to admit he has something to do with this.''

"Hey, it wasn't me who sat on a porch kissing one man and then having brunch with another the next morning.'' He wondered how *she'd* have felt if he'd shown up at her house with another woman on his arm. She wouldn't have liked it any better than he'd liked seeing her with Richard. He wanted to tell her that, but figured he'd come off sounding jealous. Hell, he *was* jealous.

"You didn't stick around long enough for me to explain.''

"What was there to say?'' It was obvious enough to Glen what had happened, and frankly he wasn't interested in hearing the details. Anyway, that was all in the past. What mattered now was the future.

"I'm flattered, Glen, that you'd ask me to marry you.''

"What do you think about the ring?'' He held it up so she could get a better view. Cal had spared no expense with this beauty, but Glen realized he'd prefer to have Ellie choose her own ring. Something unique to her. To them.

Ellie's hand closed over his. "Give the ring back to Cal.''

"I'm glad, because I'd rather the two of us shopped for one together.''

She shook her head. "I'm sorry.''

"I *said* I'd rather the two of us picked out a diamond together," he told her again, only louder.

"I heard you the first time," she said impatiently. "What I meant was that I'm sorry, but no. I can't marry you."

It took him a moment to realize what she was saying. "You're turning me down?" Each one of those words seared a hole through his heart. When he recovered from the shock, he asked, "Do you mind telling me why?" He had to know. Maybe he should have left things as they were, collected his shattered pride and gone home—but he couldn't. "I...I thought we had something special."

"We do. Friendship. You said it yourself, remember?"

He nodded.

"I don't want a husband who proposes marriage to me because it's an obligation."

"I didn't mean it like that." His voice sounded odd to his own ears. A little ragged and faraway.

"When and if I agree to marry anyone, I want it to be for specific reasons."

"Okay, that sounds fair." Weren't *his* reasons specific? Glen's ego came to the rescue, and the anger and pain in his voice were less evident now. More controlled.

"Reasons other than *it's time* and *you have excellent qualities*. Reasons other than *I should get married now and you'll do.*"

"I didn't say that!"

"No, but you might as well have. Oh, and I almost forgot, you said you *owed* me."

"Owed you what?"

"I might not get the words right so bear with me." He could tell she was being sarcastic but wasn't sure why. "Something about duty because you'd embarrassed me in front of the whole town."

"I...I didn't mean it to sound like that. Damn it, Ellie, you're putting words in my mouth."

"I don't need any favors, Glen."

He looked at her, afraid she was about to cry, but he was mistaken. Her face was strong and confident. She could give him all the excuses in the book, but he knew what was going on here and wasn't shy about saying it, either.

"It's Richard, isn't it? You're in love with him."

"That's it!" she cried.

"I thought as much." He shoved the ring back into his pocket. He'd tell his brother to bury it—the diamond must be hexed.

"The thing is, Glen, you're too late."

"Too late?" He didn't know what the hell she meant by that, but he wasn't sticking around to find out.

Ellie, however, insisted he hear her out. "Richard came by earlier and he proposed. Sorry, Glen, he beat you to the punch."

Chapter Nine

Not for a single moment would Cal describe himself as a romantic. Despite that, he felt good about encouraging his little brother to go and propose to Ellie Frasier. He'd even given him the ring!

Good enough to tell his neighbor. It wasn't often that Cal had reason to shoot the bull over a telephone; usually a beer at Billy D's served the same purpose, but even better. However, this news was too good to keep to himself.

Grady answered on the second ring.

"It's Cal," he announced.

"Something wrong?" Grady asked right off.

They'd been best friends since first grade, and Grady knew him about as well as anyone ever would. Over the years they'd been through a lot together. As kids, they'd explored Bitter End. Later Grady had talked to him about his parents' deaths, his problems with Richard, his concerns about Laredo. And it was Grady Cal had gone to when Jennifer canceled their wedding, Grady who'd gotten him home safely when he'd fallen down drunk. Grady who'd talked some sense into him when he badly needed to hear it.

"Glen's driving into town to ask Ellie to marry him," Cal said without preamble. He wasn't a man who wasted words.

"You're kidding!" Grady sounded shocked.

"No. He's been acting like a wounded bear for damn near two weeks and then I found him mumbling to himself in the barn, about as miserable as I've ever seen him. Tried to talk to him, but he damn near bit my head off. I'd had enough. I figured he should either fix what was wrong or forget Ellie."

"And Glen listened?"

"No, I didn't get the chance to give him my advice. He decided to marry her all on his own."

"That's great." Cal heard the relief in Grady's voice and knew his neighbor harbored his own set of fears when it came to Ellie Frasier. "At least she won't be marrying Richard, then."

"Not if Glen has anything to say about it." Cal knew Grady didn't trust his younger brother, and with damn good reason.

"I was thinking of celebrating," Cal continued. "You're welcome to join me if you want. There's cold beer in the fridge, plus a bottle of the hard stuff if you're interested." An invitation from Cal was about as rare as a phone call.

"I might just do that."

A couple of minutes later Cal hung up the receiver, feeling more like his old self than at any time since his broken engagement. Grinning from ear to ear, he reached for a beer and walked outside, where he leaned comfortably against the porch railing. In years past he'd spent many an evening in this very spot, looking out over the land, knowing that cattle grazed peacefully in the distance. In certain moods, wistful moods, he liked to imagine a wife standing at his side and the sound of their children's laughter echoing in the house.

Glen married.

Cal had known it would probably happen one day, and he'd always wondered how'd he react, seeing that, despite his imaginings, he'd likely remain a bachelor himself. In fact, he felt surprisingly good about having played a small role in his brother's romance. He'd known Glen was in love with Ellie months before it even occurred to Glen.

Glen's feelings for her had been apparent for a long time. He'd drive into town and return a couple of hours later and talk of little else. Ellie amused him, challenged him, comforted him. She fired his senses. And all that time Glen had insisted it was "just" friendship.

Right! Cal nearly laughed out loud. It was friendship and a whole lot more.

The sound of an engine broke into Cal's musings, and he looked toward the driveway as Grady's truck pulled into view. Good, his neighbor was going to take him up on his offer.

Grady leaped down from the pickup and raised a bottle of whiskey high above his head. "Glen getting married. Hot damn, this calls for a party," he shouted.

Cal lifted his beer in salute and let out a cheer.

"So Glen's really dong it," Grady said, taking the porch steps two at a time. "He's marrying Ellie."

"Unless the woman's a fool and turns him down."

"Ellie Frasier's no fool," Grady said with confidence.

"He took the diamond I bought Jennifer," Cal explained as he headed into the house for a couple of tumblers and some ice.

"Glen asked Ellie to marry him with Jennifer's ring?" Grady followed him, sounding worried.

"It's just a loan. I figure Ellie'll want to choose her own diamond later." He dumped the ice cubes into two mismatched glasses.

"You think that was wise?"

"Well, yeah. This way Glen wasn't proposing to her empty-handed."

The two men returned to the porch and Cal poured two

generous measures of the honey-colored liquor over the ice, but he noted that his friend's worried frown didn't go away. "What harm could it do?" he asked.

"Probably none." Grady sat down with Cal in the white wicker chairs and relaxed. Leaning back, he stretched out his long legs and crossed his ankles, then with a deep contented sigh, raised the tumbler to his lips.

Cal tasted his own drink. His eyes watered as the whiskey burned its way down his throat.

"I have to tell you," Grady admitted, "it does my heart good to know Richard's out of the picture with Ellie."

"Mine, too." Cal wasn't fond of the youngest Weston. Richard was a difficult person to understand. Witty, amiable, a natural leader—and yet he'd squandered his talents, in Cal's opinion, anyway. Richard had taken a wrong turn and he'd never gotten steered back on course. It was unfortunate, too, because he could have been a success at just about anything he chose.

"I told Savannah," Grady mentioned casually, "and she's delighted for Glen." Then, looking as though he might have done something wrong, he glanced at Cal. "You don't mind, do you?"

"She won't tell anyone else, will she?" Not that it mattered; word would be out soon enough.

"I doubt it." Grady didn't seem to know for sure.

Cal wasn't really worried, though. Savannah—sensitive and kind, the complete opposite of Richard—would never say anything to ruin another person's happiness. She'd never cheat Ellie out of the pleasure of spreading the news herself.

"Which one of us is gong to be next?" Cal asked, although he already had his suspicions. Grady. He'd seen the way his friend's eyes followed Caroline Daniels at the Cattleman's dance. Later, when she'd asked him to dance during the ladies' choice, Grady had been so thrilled he'd nearly stumbled all over himself. Not that he'd let on, but Cal knew. Yup, it'd be Grady for sure.

First Glen and then Grady. Soon all his friends would be married, and he'd be living on the ranch alone. The picture that formed in his mind was a desolate one but preferable to the thought of letting another Jennifer Healy into his life.

The sound of a vehicle barreling up the driveway caught Cal's attention.

"Glen?" Grady asked.

"I didn't expect him back so soon." Cal set his tumbler aside.

"You think everything went all right, don't you?"

"Don't know why it wouldn't." But Cal was beginning to feel some doubts, considering the speed at which Glen had been driving.

The slam of the truck door echoed through the quiet evening.

"I don't like the look of this," Grady said in a low voice.

Cal didn't, either. He dashed down the porch when he saw Glen moving toward the barn. "I wonder what happened," he said. "I'd better find out. Be back in a couple of minutes."

Cal didn't want to think about what might have gone wrong, but clearly something had. He opened the barn door and searched the dim interior. It took his eyes a moment to adjust, and when he did finally see Glen, his uneasiness intensified. His brother was pitching hay like a man possessed.

"I take it things didn't go so well between you and Ellie," Cal said, hoping he sounded casual.

"You could say that." Glen's shoulders heaved with exertion. "What's Grady doing here?"

"We're…" He almost slipped and said they were celebrating Glen's engagement. "We're just shootin' the breeze."

Silence.

"You *did* talk to Ellie?"

Glen stopped midmotion, the pitch fork full of hay. "We talked."

Cal wondered how to proceed. "Did she like the ring?" he asked, and realized immediately it was probably a tactless question.

"She didn't say."

"I see."

"I doubt it." Glen stabbed the fork into the ground, breathing hard, his face red from exertion.

"Do you want to tell me about it or would you rather work this out on your own?"

Glen took a couple of moments to think it over. "I...I don't know," he mumbled.

Another silence. Cal knew it was up to Glen to talk or not.

"I owe you an apology," Glen surprised him by saying next.

"Me? What for?"

Glen looked him full in the eye. "When Jennifer walked out on you, I was secretly glad. As far as I was concerned, you got a lucky break. I thought she wasn't the right woman for you. I didn't stop to consider how you must have felt, how damn hard her leaving was on you."

Cal didn't quite understand how all this talk about Jennifer applied to the current situation, but he didn't want to interrupt Glen.

"Hurt like hell, didn't it?"

Cal wasn't going to deny it. "At the time it did. I don't think about it much anymore."

Glen reached into his pocket for the diamond that had once belonged to Cal's ex-fiancée. He stared at it for several seconds. "I wonder how long it'll take me to forget Ellie," he said, sounding as if he was speaking to himself.

He raised his head as he handed Cal back the ring, and the look in his eyes spoke of blinding pain.

"Ellie's decided to marry Richard Weston."

NOT ONCE HAD ELLIE SAID she'd *accepted* Richard Weston's proposal, but that was what Glen had immediately assumed. It hurt that he'd actually believe she would marry anyone else when it should be clear as creek water that she was in love with him!

She let herself into her house and slumped down on the sofa, discouraged and depressed. She'd always known that Glen wasn't much of a romantic, but she'd hoped he could at least propose marriage without making it sound like an insult. He'd said all the wrong things. He'd talked about an obligation to "take care" of her; well, no thanks, she could take care of herself. He'd said it was "time" he got married—so what did that have to do with her? He'd referred to her "excellent qualities" as though he was interviewing her for a job! Perhaps worst of all, he'd half admitted that his sudden desire to propose had been prompted by his effort to outdo Richard Weston.

The one thing he'd never said was that he loved her.

Crossing her arms, she leaned her head back and closed her eyes. It was at times like this that she missed her father most. He always seemed to know what to do, and Ellie feared that in her anger she'd badly bungled her relationship with Glen. She feared that nothing would ever be the same again.

She knew about the lottery at Billy D's and all the Texas two-step jokes. She hated the idea of being in the middle of some stupid male rivalry, and everything Glen said only reinforced that. It bothered her, too, that he'd come to her with a used engagement ring, a leftover from his brother's failed romance. She'd drawn the only sensible conclusion, which was that he'd been in such a rush to get to her before

Richard proposed, he hadn't taken the time to buy his own ring.

Now she didn't know what to do. She loved Glen and wanted more than anything to be his wife, but at the same time she needed to feel that she was more to him than a trophy, a way of triumphing over Richard. Deciding to marry someone wasn't like switching dance partners—even in the Texas two-step!

She needed Glen to acknowledge that he loved her, and she needed to understand that his feelings for her had nothing to do with Richard. She wanted Glen to look into his heart.

But she worried he wouldn't be able to see beyond his own disappointments.

GLEN SAT AT THE BREAKFAST table and stared glumly at the kitchen wall, sipping his coffee. It was barely five and he was already on his third cup.

Cal ambled down the stairs, yawning loudly. "You're up early," he muttered as he headed for the coffeepot.

Glen didn't tell his brother that he hadn't been to sleep yet. He'd gone to bed and closed his eyes, but it'd done no good. He'd finally gotten up at three-thirty and sat waiting for the tightness in his chest to go away so he could breathe without this pain.

"You feeling all right?" Cal asked.

His brother was more awake than Glen had given him credit for. "I'm fine."

Cal leaned against the kitchen counter, holding his coffee mug with both hands, and studied Glen.

"I said I was fine," Glen said a bit more gruffly than he intended. He wasn't up to talking. In time the details would come out, the same way they had when Jennifer canceled the wedding. Cal had been tight-lipped for weeks, then gradually, bit by bit, Glen had pieced it all together until he had a fairly accurate picture of the events that led up to the final scene.

Cal's face seemed to darken. "It doesn't seem either one of us is the marrying kind," he said, then pushed away from the counter and left the house.

His eyes burning from lack of sleep, Glen toyed with the idea of taking the day off, but instinctively realized that would be his worst choice. He needed to stay busy. Otherwise thoughts of Ellie and Richard would drive him crazy.

Downing the last of his coffee, he followed Cal.

The day dragged. Glen had never felt wearier in body and spirit. By late afternoon he knew the only way to find peace was to seek out Richard Weston and congratulate him. Then he'd talk to Ellie and wish her and Richard every happiness. He was sincere about that; he loved her enough to want her to have a good life.

He didn't tell Cal where he was going when he was finished for the day. Nor did he bother to shower or shave.

Cal had just ridden in when Glen was ready to leave.

"Did Ellie mention anything about the wire cutters I ordered?" Cal asked, stopping him.

Glen froze at the mention of her name. He might as well get used to it. She was as much a part of his everyday life as this ranch.

"I'll ask her if you want," Glen said.

Cal looked as if he wanted to say something, but hesitated. Then, "I didn't mean...I forgot."

"Don't worry about it. Frasier's has been our supplier for a lot of years and I don't think we should change things now." He was man enough to accept being rejected, or he'd like to believe he was, anyway.

Ellie, ever sensitive and thoughtful, was probably worried about him. That would be just like her. Glen didn't want her to think her decision had ruined their relationship.

They could still be friends. Sort of. Not the way they'd been in the past but...friendly.

Glen headed for the Weston place. He found Richard loading supplies into the back of Grady's pickup when he arrived. The other man looked mildly surprised when Glen sought him out. He stood there with a case of canned goods balanced on his shoulder, his stance defensive.

"You wanted to talk to me?" Richard asked.

"I came to congratulate you." No need to hedge. This wasn't a conversation he relished having, and the sooner he'd finished the better.

"Congratulate me?" Richard echoed. "Did I win the lottery and someone forgot to tell me?"

Glen didn't appreciate the joke. "In a manner of speaking."

Richard leaned forward and dumped the box onto the open tailgate. "What's up, Patterson?"

"It's about you and Ellie."

Richard scowled. "What about us?"

"I understand you asked her to marry you."

"What of it?"

"I also understand that she's accepted."

Richard had started to remove his gloves, one finger at a time. His head snapped up at Glen's statement. "Ellie's a hell of a woman, isn't she? I didn't realize she'd decided to let the word out." He nudged Glen with his elbow. "But then, that's just like my Ellie."

My Ellie. The words hurt like alcohol on a cut, and Glen flinched before he could hide his reaction. Recovering quickly, he forced a smile. "I couldn't agree with you more," he said. "Ellie's one of a kind."

Richard slapped him hard on the back. "I guess you could say the best man won."

"Yeah, I guess you could say that," Glen answered, clenching his teeth.

"I don't suppose she happened to mention a wedding date, did she?" He laughed. "Seems the groom's always the last to know."

"Can't say as she did."

"It'll be soon, if I have anything to say about it." Richard hopped onto the tailgate, his legs dangling. "The wedding will be a small intimate affair right here in Savannah's rose garden. Family and a few friends. You're invited of course."

"Thank you."

"Hey, no problem." Richard began whistling; Glen might not have much of an ear for music; but he recognized the "Wedding March."

He tried not to let it distract him. "I want to wish you both every happiness," he said formally.

"That's good of you, Glen, and I appreciate it. I'm sure Ellie will, too." Richard thrust out his hand. "I realize it was difficult for you to lose her, but I want you to know, I plan to make Ellie happy. The two of us would like to consider you a friend."

"I hope you will." This was what made Richard so damn difficult to understand, Glen mused. One minute he was a jackass; the next, he was a regular joe. "If you need anything, give me a call," he offered.

"I will."

Glen climbed back into his pickup. Despite his dislike of Richard, he felt better for having cleared the air between them. Although he'd dreaded talking to the guy, he was glad now that he had.

He hoped everything would go as well with Ellie.

The ache in his gut intensified as he drove into town. When he entered the feed store, she was ringing up a sale for Lyle Whitehouse. She didn't notice Glen until she handed Lyle his package. Her hand froze in midair and she gaped at him as if she couldn't believe her eyes. Recovering quickly, she released the bag.

Lyle turned around, and when he saw Glen, he grinned broadly. Then he winked and gave him a thumbs-up as he walked out of the store.

"Hello, Glen," Ellie said tentatively.

"Ellie." He nodded once. "Cal wanted me to ask you about those wire cutters he ordered."

"They won't be in until Monday," she said, sounding oddly breathless.

"I'll tell him." He felt awkward and tongue-tied again, the way he had when he proposed. He waited a moment, just staring at her. "I have a few things to say. Is now a good time?"

"As good as any," she said stiffly. She remained on her side of the counter while he stayed on the other.

Damn she was beautiful. That wasn't the kind of thing he should be thinking, he told himself, and glanced away. "First, all I really want is for you to be happy."

"I am happy," she said a little too loudly.

"Good."

Ellie moved out from behind the cash register and started restacking blocks of salt.

"I was hoping we could remain friendly," he said, moving up behind her.

"I was hoping that, too."

Glen raised his hands to place them on her shoulders, the need to touch her almost impossible to resist. He paused, then with unprecedented determination dropped his arms to his sides. He had no right to touch Ellie anymore. She was engaged to another man.

"You've been my closest and dearest friend," she whispered, and turned to face him. "I don't know what I would've done without you when Dad was so terribly ill…and since."

Glen wasn't sure if she'd come toward him or if he'd stepped toward her, but all at once they were standing mere inches apart. Their eyes avoided meeting, but their slow labored breathing seemed to keep pace.

"I needed you," she whispered, "and you were there for me."

Again he reminded himself that she was engaged to Richard, and yet all he could think about was kissing her one last time. Just one kiss, to tell her goodbye, to wish her well.

Everything within him yearned for her. It seemed natural to stand this close; it seemed even more natural to hold her, but he managed to resist. He mustn't feel these things any longer, mustn't allow himself to look at her this way. Mustn't kiss her again.

His heart went wild when Ellie stepped into his arms. When she raised her lips to his. Her kiss nearly buckled his knees. It began as a simple, almost chaste touch, her warm mouth on his. Unfortunately it didn't stay chaste long. Glen slipped his arm around her waist and against every dictate of common sense, urged her closer. If this was to be their last kiss, then he'd make sure it was one they'd both remember.

The kiss spoke far more eloquently of his need and love for her than any words he'd ever uttered. Ellie moaned and he cradled her face with both hands. The kiss grew molten-hot and would have grown hotter had they continued. Abruptly Glen released her, trembling with the restraint it demanded to pull away.

She stared at him, wide-eyed, then pressed the back of her hand against her mouth.

"I suppose you're waiting for an apology," he said, knowing that kiss should never have happened. "I'll give you one if you insist, but it'd be a bold-faced lie. This is only the third time we've kissed, and it's the last. It has to be.'' He reached out to stroke her hair and whispered, ''Be happy, Ellie. Be very happy.''

Looking as if she'd been struck dumb, she continued to stand there, staring up at him.

''Richard doesn't deserve you,'' he said, his voice gruff with pain, ''but I don't, either.'' He touched her cheek, loving the feel of her skin beneath his fingertips. Then he turned and walked out of the store.

ELLIE DIDN'T MOVE for five solid minutes after he left. Her hand remained poised at her lips, the taste and feel of him still clinging to her mouth.

Little of what he'd said made any sense—but they hadn't been able to communicate effectively in weeks. Except when they kissed…. They'd been best friends for years, able to talk about anything, and then overnight it had all changed.

The big oaf. He'd screwed up his marriage proposal and now he was back, kissing her senseless and saying the most beautiful words she'd ever heard. He hadn't actually said he loved her, although his kiss was pretty persuasive. What he'd said was, ''Be happy.'' And if he didn't love her, he wouldn't have told her that. Because Glen Patterson was an honest man.

Glen's kiss still lingered on her lips when Richard casually sauntered into the store.

''Darling,'' he said, flashing her an easy smile. He grabbed her in a bear hug and soundly kissed her cheek.

Furious, Ellie wiped away his kiss, not wanting his touch to taint what she'd shared with Glen. ''Let go of me,'' she ordered. One thing she detested was being manhandled. When Richard didn't immediately comply, she elbowed him hard in the ribs.

''Ouch,'' he muttered, holding her at arm's length. ''Why didn't you tell me yourself?''

"Tell you what?"

"That you'd decided to accept my proposal." He glared at her as if suddenly aware that something wasn't right.

"Who told you that?" Although she could almost predict his answer.

"Glen Patterson," he murmured. "It's all a joke, isn't it?" His lip curled into a snarl.

She *was* going to kill Glen, no doubt about it. "Not a joke," she said feeling genuinely sorry, "but a misunderstanding."

"Well, that's just fine," Richard spit. "I just went and bought myself a new suit for the wedding."

"Oh, Richard." She brought one hand to her mouth. "Glen didn't understand—"

"What the hell am I supposed to do about the suit?" He actually made it sound as though they should get married because of a new set of clothes.

"Can you return it?"

"I don't think so," he said, his voice tight with anger.

"I am sorry, Richard."

He looked as if he wanted to plow his fist through something. "It wouldn't have worked, anyway," he said. "You're too uptight. Making love to you would have been like warming up an ice cube."

Ellie had heard all she cared to. "I think you should go. And take your insults with you."

"Fine. Whatever. Patterson really had me fooled— he must've enjoyed playing me for an idiot. Tell him I'm not going to forget his sick joke." That said, he bolted out the door.

If Glen's actions earlier had confused her, Richard's outraged her. She hadn't missed the threat, but as far as she knew, Glen had nothing to fear from Richard Weston. He should worry about what *she* planned to do to him, instead.

George, who'd gone on an errand, was back fifteen

minutes later. The minute he walked into the store, Ellie reached for her truck keys. "I have to go," she said. "Can you close up shop for me?"

"I...I guess."

It wasn't like her to walk out before five, but it couldn't be helped. She was in her truck and headed out of town in five minutes flat. She managed the forty-minute drive in thirty; half an hour was not long enough to cool her anger even slightly.

Glen and Cal must have heard her coming because both men stepped onto the porch when she arrived. She glared at Glen with undisguised fury.

"Ellie, is something wrong?" he asked, walking down the steps toward her.

With her hands planted on her hips, she yelled, "Did you actually believe for one minute I was going to marry Richard Weston?"

He hesitated, fifteen or so feet away. "That's what you said."

"I said," she returned from between clenched teeth, "that Richard had proposed. I did *not,* I repeat, *not* at any time state that I'd accepted his proposal of marriage."

Glen's face was stricken. "You didn't?"

"I most certainly did not. Furthermore, anyone with eyes in his head would know it's *you* I love."

"You love me?"

"Don't pretend you didn't know, Glen Patterson. I've loved you forever." But at the moment she wasn't particularly happy about it.

"Then you'll marry me, right?" Glen looked like he was about to fly across the yard and haul her into his arms.

Ellie stopped him cold in his tracks. "Give me one good reason why I'd want to marry a man who's got the brains of a tumbleweed."

"She loves you, all right," Cal shouted from the porch steps.

"You stay out of this," Ellie shouted back, pointing an accusing finger at Glen's brother. "You encouraged him to do it, didn't you?"

"Yup." Cal seemed downright proud of himself.

"The next time Glen asks you for advice, ignore him." Then she threw open the truck door and climbed inside.

"Ellie!" Glen started toward her. But when she revved the engine, he apparently knew better than to press his luck. He stayed where he was. Good thing, because in her current frame of mind she was liable to run him over.

When the dust had died down, Ellie glanced in her rear-view mirror and groaned. Cal and Glen Patterson were leaping about, hugging each other wildly.

Chapter Ten

Glen Patterson had never been happier. Ellie loved him. *Him*. Not Richard Weston. And by golly, she was going to marry him, too!

"I knew it," Cal announced cheerfully, as though he was personally responsible for the unexpected turn of events.

"Did you ever see such a woman?" Glen asked, watching Ellie drive away. Damn, but she had spunk. It wasn't every woman who would've come out here to confront him the way she had.

Cal chuckled. "Don't think I've ever seen a female that mad." He glanced at his brother. "How're you going to get her to marry you?"

That was a question Glen hadn't considered. Of course Ellie would marry him. She loved him. He loved her. Marriage was the natural result of such feelings. Sure, she was mad at him right now, but she'd cool off and they'd sit down and talk this out and plan for their future together. "Any suggestions?"

"From me?" Cal adamantly shook his head. "Didn't you hear? Ellie wasn't too impressed with the advice I gave you earlier, although I don't know what I said that was so wrong. Do you?"

"Nope." Women baffled him just as much as they did Cal. "So, who should I ask for advice?"

Cal thought it over a moment. "Mom?"

"Not Mom," Glen said. He loved his mother, but she was sure to meddle. All mothers did. Once she heard about this, she'd want to fix it; she'd want to talk to Ellie and act as a go-between and generally get involved. Glen shuddered. He preferred to handle the situation himself.

Cal shrugged. "Dovie, then. She's got a good head on her shoulders."

"Dovie," Glen repeated slowly. Yes. She was a good choice.

After a night without sleep, followed by one of the most emotionally draining days of his life, Glen nearly nodded off during dinner. As soon as the evening chores were done, he showered and went to bed. He'd figure out what he should say to Ellie. Tomorrow... He'd figure it out tomorrow. As he drifted into sleep, he actually felt happy for the first time in weeks.

The next afternoon Glen opened the door to Dovie's Antiques. Glancing around, he immediately removed his hat. Little wonder the women in town loved this place. It was full to the rafters with pretty things, and smelled a little like Savannah's garden. If his nose didn't mislead him, he caught the scent of some mighty fine brandy, too. Must be what she used to make that famous cordial of hers.

"Hello, Glen." Dovie was her usual lighthearted self. "What can I do for you this fine day?"

"Ah..." For the life of him, Glen couldn't think of a single way to start the conversation.

Dovie regarded him expectantly. "I'll have you know, young man, I have my money riding on you."

"I beg your pardon?"

"Do you think only the men are in on Billy D's lottery?"

"Oh, that." Glen had forgotten all about that silly lottery. He stood just inside the door, arms tight against his sides, for fear one wrong move would send hundreds of fragile little things tumbling to the floor.

"Come on inside, Glen," Dovie encouraged. "You aren't going to break anything."

He took a few cautious steps, then glanced anxiously around the store and back at Dovie.

"Is there a problem?" she asked with concern.

Glen had always liked his mother's friend. It was Dovie who'd suggested the bed-and-breakfast idea and who'd helped his mother decorate the old Howe Mansion.

"I need some advice," he finally said. The last time he'd been this unsure of himself—not counting the day he proposed to Ellie—was when he'd roped his first calf in the Brewster rodeo at the age of ten.

"The advice is free, but the tea will cost you a dollar."

"Tea?"

"I think best when I'm sitting down." Smiling, Dovie motioned toward the assembled tables and chairs in one corner of the shop.

"All right," he agreed.

"I take it this all has to do with Ellie?" Dovie asked, leading him to a small table covered by a pretty floral cloth.

"You know, then."

"I know you and Richard made first-class fools of yourselves at the dance."

Glen wished folks would forget about that. "It's gotten worse since."

Dovie carried a blue-and-white china teapot and two cups to the table. "I was afraid of that."

"Cal suggested I talk to you about Ellie. You see, I want us to get married. I tried asking her and it didn't turn out the way I'd hoped. Can you help me?"

"I can try." Dovie poured him some tea, then served herself. "Milk? Sugar? Lemon?"

Glen shook his head mutely. He generally sweetened his

tea, but he wasn't willing to do it with one of those miniature silver spoons. He already felt like an oversize buffoon in this dainty little shop.

"How would you like me to advise you?" Dovie asked.

"Can you tell me what I can say to convince Ellie to marry me?"

Dovie frowned slightly. "Perhaps you should tell me how you proposed the first time."

Glen recalled what he could of their conversation. "Best I can remember, she started getting hostile when I mentioned I felt responsible for embarrassing her at the dance."

Dovie nodded, and Glen continued, "I told her I admired her and I wanted to marry her. That was when I brought out the diamond ring I borrowed from Cal."

"You *borrowed* an engagement ring?"

"Just so I'd have something to offer. I wanted Ellie to know I was serious, and a man doesn't get more serious than diamonds."

Dovie was frowning again.

"Was that so terrible?" Glen demanded. "All I want is for Ellie to know how much I love her."

"Why don't we start with telling her that this time?" Dovie suggested.

"Ellie already knows how I feel about her." It was incomprehensible to him that she wouldn't. He'd made himself the laughingstock of the entire town over her. When she'd rejected his marriage proposal, he'd swallowed his pride and wished her happiness, even at the cost of his own. A man didn't say those kinds of things to a woman he didn't love. "She's *got* to know," he added.

"A woman likes to hear the words, Glen."

It was that simple? Of course he loved Ellie, and if all he had to do was tell her how much... He reached for his hat and got eagerly to his feet. "Great. I'll let her know right now."

Dovie grabbed his shirtsleeve. "I'm not finished yet."

"Oh." He sat back down.

"Is there anything else you plan to tell Ellie?"

Glen wasn't sure he understood the question. Perplexed, he gave it a moment's thought. "Just that I can't get married next Tuesday because the farrier's coming."

"Oh, dear." Dovie briefly closed her eyes.

"That's the wrong thing to say?"

"Well…yes."

"Thursday's not good, either. I play poker at Billy D's on Thursdays, but I'd be wiling to give that up if Ellie decided she wanted to get married then."

"Have you considered that Ellie might want a church wedding?"

He hadn't, and the mere suggestion made his blood run cold. All this time he'd been thinking they'd fly off to Vegas and get married the same night. A quickie wedding, because now that the decision had been made, he was ready. Strike while the iron's hot, as the farrier might say.

"Besides, I think you might be getting ahead of yourself," Dovie murmured. "First you've got to convince Ellie to be your bride."

"Right." If the truth be known, he'd given more thought to the honeymoon than the wedding. He was in love, and damn it all, he wanted to make love to Ellie. "Why does this have to be so complicated?" he wanted to know. "I love her, and she's already confessed she loves me."

Sighing, he took a careful sip of his cooling tea. "When she was going through her father's things, she found this old Bible passed down from his family," Glen said, thinking out loud. "She showed it to me and turned to the page where her family's names and dates are listed. Weddings, deaths, births—you know. All day, I've been thinking about Ellie and me entering our names in that Bible, and someday, God willing, writing down the names of our children. I love Ellie, and it's a love that'll last all our lives. Maybe a hundred years from now one of our great-great grandchildren will come upon that Bible and wonder about us. I'd want them to know—just from the way we lived— that despite everything life threw at us, our love survived.''

"Oh, Glen, that's beautiful," Dovie said softly, and squeezed his hand.

"It was?"

"Tell Ellie that."

"About putting our names in her family Bible?"

"Yes. Speak from your heart and don't mention the farrier, all right?"

"I'll do it." Glen felt immeasurably better.

GRADY RELAXED against the back of a molded plastic bench in the bowling alley. Lloyd Bonney had asked if he'd substitute for him the next two weeks while he was on vacation. It'd been ages since Grady had last bowled, but Lloyd was a likeable guy and he hated to turn him down. That wasn't the only reason, either; for the first time in six years, he was able to indulge himself with a few leisure activities. He used to enjoy bowling and had been fairly good at it.

He was a bit rusty, but he'd bowled a decent series tonight. It felt good to be with friends, to laugh again. Finally he had the financial security and the extra time to make it possible. This evening had whetted his appetite for more.

He was on his way to Billy D's afterward when Max Jordan followed him outside.

"Grady, you got a moment?"

"Sure."

Max shifted his gaze away from Grady. "Listen, I realize this is a bad time and all, but I need to talk to you about Richard."

"Yeah?" Grady didn't like the sound of this.

"He charged a few things at my store—clothes and boots—when he first came back to town and he hasn't paid me and...well, it's been almost three months now."

Grady's grip tightened on his bowling bag. "How much does he owe you?"

Max stated an amount that made Grady's stomach clench. His brother must have picked out the most expensive clothes in the store.

"Earlier this week he charged a new suit," Max continued. "It's a pricey one, and—"

"You let him do that even when he hadn't paid you for the other things?" Grady was furious with his brother, and with Max, too.

Max lowered his eyes to the pavement. "I feel like an old fool now. Richard stopped in the store and told me he was getting married. I was pleased for him and Ellie. It wasn't until later that I learned they weren't engaged, at all."

"It isn't your fault." Grady blamed himself as much as anyone. It'd been a mistake to let Richard stay at the ranch for even one night. He knew the kind of man his brother was, and still he'd allowed Richard to take advantage of him. Well, no more. He was sending that bastard packing.

"I'll take the suit back," Max said.

"I'll personally see that he returns it," Grady told him. "I can't tell you how bad I feel about all this."

"And the other money he owes? Richard had me put it on the family account, but so far I've mailed all the bills to him."

"I'll make sure he takes care of it right away," Grady pledged. Richard would pay one way or another, he decided. He should have realized sooner what was happening. His no-good brother arrives in town, throws himself a party and buys some fancy duds to go along with everything else.

Max Jordan wasn't the old fool; Grady was. Why hadn't he guessed where Richard's clothes had come from? Why hadn't he known Richard would pull something like this?

The evening that had started out with such promise was ruined. Grady changed his mind about meeting his friends for a beer and headed directly back to the ranch, instead. He was having this out with Richard once and for all.

The lights in the house were off when Grady got home. He attacked the stairs with a vengeance and didn't bother to knock on his brother's door. It shouldn't have surprised him to find the bed empty, but for some reason it did. Although it was about midnight, Richard wasn't anywhere to be found. Why the hell shouldn't he party half the night, seeing as he hadn't done a lick of work all day, or any day since he arrived? Grady resisted the temptation to slam the door shut.

He lay awake half the night, listening for his brother's return. Eventually he'd fallen asleep and never did hear him come home. But then, Richard seemed to have a sixth sense about such things; even as a child, he'd been able to smell trouble and avoid it.

In the morning another check of his brother's room showed that Richard hadn't been home that night.

"Have you seen Richard lately?" he asked his sister when he went downstairs for breakfast.

Savannah shook her head. "He's probably still sleeping."

"His bed is empty." Grady used his fork to grab a pancake from the stack in the middle of the table. "When you see him, tell him I need to talk to him, all right?"

"Problems?"

Grady didn't want to involve Savannah in this, but she knew him too well not to realize something was wrong. He tried distancing her with another question. "Did Laredo leave the house already?"

"What's Richard done?" Savannah asked, ignoring the question.

Grady sighed and set down the jar of maple syrup. "Max Jordan talked to me last night about some money Richard owes him. Apparently our dear little brother has charged a few things at Max's he hasn't bothered to pay for."

Savannah didn't comment, but he saw sadness on her face.

"It makes me wonder if he's been doing the same thing with anyone else in town." Grady grabbed another pancake and picked up the syrup again.

"He has," Savannah confessed in a small voice.

"And you knew about it?"

"I…" She bit her lip. "I just found out about it myself. Millie Greenville talked to me last week. She suggested that perhaps we could trade something for the money Richard owes her. My roses, for example."

Grady slammed the syrup jar down. "You didn't agree to this, did you?"

"No."

"Good."

"But—"

"I won't hear of it, Savannah, and neither will Laredo. Richard's the one who owes that money, not you and not me. He's going to repay it, too, if it's the last thing he ever does. Every penny."

"I know," she said. "Laredo and I've already discussed what to do, and he's as adamant as you are."

Grady's fork sliced viciously across the pancake. He forced himself to relax, knowing his anger would ultimately hurt him far more than it would Richard.

Laredo had saddled the horses and was waiting for him outside when he finished his meal. Savannah walked out, too, and with an agility Grady envied, her husband leaned over his horse's neck and kissed her.

"If Richard shows up, tell him..." Grady paused, then shook his head. "Don't tell him anything. Let me do the talking this time."

Savannah nodded. "He's been making himself scarce lately."

"Now we know why, don't we?"

The sadness was back in his sister's eyes before she turned away and hurried into the house.

RICHARD DOMINATED Grady's thoughts for the rest of the day. By the time he got home, he was ready to read his brother the riot act. To his surprise Richard was there waiting for him.

"I understand you want to talk to me," his brother said.

Grady was so angry he needed every bit of self-control not to explode with it. "Damn right I want to talk to you."

"It's about the stuff I charged in town, isn't it?"

"Yes. I can't believe you'd take advantage of our good name to—"

"Listen, Grady, you've got every right to be mad, but I don't need a lecture."

"That's too bad because—"

"Before you get all bent out of shape, let me say something. I've been sick with worry about those charges. Ask Savannah if you don't believe me. I have some money owed to me, quite a bit as it happens—you know that. It was supposed to have been mailed to me long before this." He frowned thoughtfully. "It must have been misdirected. I've spent weeks trying to track it down."

If anyone knew what it was like to be low on cash, it was Grady, but he wasn't falling for his brother's lies again. He opened his mouth to tell him so when Richard continued.

"I figured I'd have those bills paid off before now. I haven't charged anything in weeks."

"What about the suit?" Grady flared.

His brother's expression became pained. "That was a...mistake. I was tricked into thinking Ellie had agreed to marry me and didn't learn until later it wasn't true." He inhaled sharply. "In my excitement I went down and bought myself a decent suit for the wedding."

"Max said he'd let you return it."

Richard smiled slightly. "As it happens the money was at the post office when I picked up the mail this afternoon. The first thing I did was pay off all the bills." He slid his hands into his jeans pockets. "I realize it was a mistake not to discuss this with you earlier."

"Yes, it was." Grady's relief was tremendous. The problem was solved and the family's good name redeemed. And none of the business owners was losing any money.

"I'm sorry you had to find out about it the way you did."

While reassured that the money matters had been properly dealt with, Grady wasn't willing to make any further allowances for his brother. Richard had worn out his welcome. "Now that your money's here, you'll be reimbursing me—and then moving on, right?"

"Yes. I appreciate you letting me stay this long. I know it's been an inconvenience, but I didn't have anywhere else to go. We've had our problems over the years, and I'm hoping we can put those behind us now." He held out his hand for Grady to shake.

Grady accepted it, glad to see that his brother had revealed the maturity to confront him man to man.

Perhaps there was hope for Richard, after all.

ELLIE HAD BEEN RESTLESS all day. With the big Fourth of July weekend coming up, business was slower than it had been in weeks. She found herself waiting, watching, hoping to see Glen—and was furious with herself for caring.

She was finished with men, Ellie told herself. She'd

rather herd goats than be married, but even as she entertained the thought, she realized it was a lie. Although she was fond of Savannah's goats, she was more than fond of Glen Patterson. Not that he deserved her affections!

Once the store had closed for the day, she returned home. The afternoon heat was intense, so she made herself some iced tea. She tugged her shirt free of her waistband, propped her bare feet on the coffee table and let the fan cool her. But it was going to take more than a fan and a glass of iced tea to revive her sagging spirits.

Because of the fan's drone she didn't hear her doorbell. When she finally realized someone was at her door, she got to her feet and hurried across the room. She threw open the door and on the other side of the screen was the largest bouquet of flowers she'd laid eyes on. While she couldn't see the man behind it, she could easily identify him by his boots.

Glen.

He waited a moment, then peeked behind the flowers and beamed her a smile. That slow sexy smile of his, capable of melting the hardest hearts, the strongest wills.

"Hello, sweetheart," he said, his smile growing wider. "Aren't you going to let me in?"

Wordlessly she unlatched the screen door and opened it for him.

He carried in the flowers and set them in the middle of her coffee table. They towered over it, filling the room with a profusion of glorious scents. Then he kissed her cheek and said, "I'll be right back."

When he returned, his arms were laden with gifts. She noted the chocolates, the basket of exotic fruit, the bottle of champagne. He set everything down next to the flowers and added three wrapped gifts.

"What's all this?" she asked, glancing at the table and then at him.

"Bribes," he said, looking very pleased with himself.

"For what?"

"I'll get to that in a moment." Taking her by the shoulders, he guided her back to the sofa. "Sit," he instructed.

She complied before she realized she should have made at least a token protest about being ordered around, but curiosity won her over.

"Here," he said, handing her the smallest of the wrapped gifts. "Open this one first."

Christmas didn't yield this many presents. "Don't think you can buy my love, Mr. Patterson."

"I don't need to, Ms. Frasier," he said confidently. "You already admitted you love me."

For the fleetest of seconds Ellie wanted to argue, tell him she'd been emotionally distraught at the time, but it was the truth—she did love him.

Inside the package she found a pen. An attractive looking ballpoint pen. Puzzled, she raised questioning eyes to him.

"Do you like it?" he asked.

"It's very nice," she said, puzzled but nevertheless excited. Before she had time to say anything more, he thrust another package at her. "This one is next." He knelt on the floor beside the sofa while she unwrapped a shoe-size box.

"Are you going to tell me what this is all about?" she asked. She tore away the paper and stared in utter amazement at the mismatched items inside.

The first thing she pulled out was a Cal Ripkin baseball card. Next she removed a shoelace, followed by rose-scented bath salts from Dovie's store, and, last, an ordinary key. Ellie examined each thing again, wondering what she was missing. As far as she could tell, the items weren't linked in any way.

"Is there a reason you're giving me one shoelace?"

He grinned. "It's blue."

She would have described it as a dark navy, closer to black—but that was beside the point. "The key?" she asked, holding that up next.

"That's to Bob Little's vacation home on the Gulf."

"Why do you have it?"

"I borrowed it," he replied, as though that answered the question.

"I see." But she didn't. Changing tactics, she reached for the pen. "What about this?"

He gazed into her eyes. "The pen is for something special. I was hoping we'd use it to write our names in that old family Bible of yours. Maybe Wade should do it for us after the wedding ceremony, but then—" He stopped abruptly and leaned back on his heels. "I'm doing this all wrong again, aren't I?" Not giving her time to answer, he continued, "I spoke with Dovie earlier and she advised me how to go about this, but now I've forgotten almost everything."

"You spoke to Dovie?"

He ignored her question. "Honest to goodness, Ellie, I don't know what I said that was so terrible when I asked you to marry me before, but whatever it was I couldn't be sorrier. I love you. I mean that."

"I know." She felt tears brimming in her eyes. She'd waited a long time for Glen to tell her how he felt.

"You do?" His relief was evident. "Dovie said I needed to tell you that, but I was sure you already knew. And I want it understood that my proposal doesn't have anything to do with the bets Billy D's taking over who you're going to marry."

"I'd forgotten about that."

"I had, too, until Dovie reminded me. I love you, Ellie," he said again.

"I know, but it doesn't hurt to say the words every now and then. Or to hear them."

"Dovie said the same thing." He brightened at that, then clasped both her hands in his and got back on his knees. "Will you marry me, Ellie?" he asked solemnly.

When she didn't immediately respond, he reached for the box she'd just opened. "I wanted to be kind of traditional about this," he said. "The baseball card is something old. I've had it since I was in junior high. The scented bath salts is something new. The key's something borrowed, since Bob said we could use his house on the Gulf for our honeymoon. And the shoelace is something blue."

"Oh, Glen."

"I'm miserable without you. Nothing seems right."

It hadn't been right for her, either.

"I know Dovie said I shouldn't mention this, but I want you to know that even though we've waited two months for the farrier's appointment, I'd cancel it if you decided Tuesday was the day you wanted to get married. I'm that crazy about you."

"You're sure this isn't because of Richard."

"Yes," he said firmly. "Very sure. Although I'm grateful to him, otherwise I don't know how long it would've taken me to realize I love you."

"Then I'm grateful to Richard, too."

"We'll buy an engagement ring together, anything you want. Only please don't make me wait much longer." His eyes filled with such hopeful expectation she couldn't have denied him anything. "Ellie, you're my friend, the best friend I've ever had. I want you to be my lover, too. My wife. The mother of my kids. I want us to grow old together."

Rather than respond with words, Ellie wrapped her arms about his neck and lowered her mouth to his. She'd yearned for this from the moment he first kissed her. She understood now, with all her heart, what poets meant when they wrote about being completed by a lover, a spouse. She felt that. He completed her life.

Glen placed his arms around her waist and pulled her from the sofa so that she was kneeling on the floor with him. They kissed again and again, each kiss more fervent than the last.

"I hope," he said, drawing back from her a fraction, "that this means yes."

"Mmm. Kiss me."

"I have every intention of kissing you for the rest of our lives."

"That sounds nice." And it did. She tightened her arms around his neck. "What's in the other box?"

"It's for the honeymoon," he mumbled.

"You were sure of yourself, weren't you?"

"No," he countered, nibbling her neck. "I was a nervous wreck. We *are* getting married, aren't we?"

"Oh, yes." She sighed as his hands closed over her breasts. "Married," she repeated, liking the sound of it.

"We're going to have a good life together," Glen whispered. He kissed her. "I promise." Another small kiss. "I'm crazy about you, Ellie."

Ellie grinned. "You already said that. But for the record, I'm crazy about you, too."

She pressed her lips to his.

Chapter Eleven

Time was running out and Richard knew it. He had to leave Promise and soon. It wouldn't take Grady more than a few days to discover there *was* no money. The check Richard had given him was written on a closed account; it was going to bounce like a rubber ball, and when Grady found out... Nor would he be able to hold off paying his creditors much longer. All he needed was a week or so to get everything ready. No one would think to look for him in that old ghost town. He'd just quietly disappear.

Until then, he had to keep the wool pulled over his brother's eyes. Even if it meant doing work he'd sworn he'd never do again. That morning Grady had insisted Richard fill in for one of his summer hands who'd suddenly taken ill. This time Grady wouldn't listen to any excuses, and Richard was forced into what he considered slave labor.

"I don't know how much good I'm going to be," he told Laredo as he saddled Roanie.

"A little extra help is all Grady is looking for," Laredo said.

Savannah's husband hadn't made any effort to disguise his dislike of him. It hadn't bothered Richard to this point. He wasn't a big fan of Laredo's, either, although he had to admire the way the wrangler had finessed himself a partnership with Grady. Smith had apparently sold some land in Oklahoma and was investing it in stock for their quarter-horse operation. There'd been a celebration the day Laredo discovered his newly purchased mare was pregnant with Renegade's foal. From all the fuss, anyone might assume it was Savannah who was pregnant, not some horse.

"Grady wants us to weigh calves and get them into the holding pens," Laredo said as they rode toward the pasture.

"What for?" Richard demanded, bouncing in the saddle. He'd never been able to get comfortable on a horse. If he was going to be working his butt off, quite literally, then he wanted an explanation of his duties.

"They need to be weighed."

"Is he selling them?"

"Eventually. He wants to be sure they're healthy and gaining weight the way they should before we send them to market."

Richard stifled a groan. Anyone looking at those smelly animals could see they were doing fine. Better than he was, Richard thought bitterly. Already his backside hurt. By the end of the day he was bound to have blisters in places people didn't normally talk about—but then that was exactly what Grady had planned.

His brother was punishing him, Richard knew, for Grady was vindictive and a sore loser. He'd been jealous of Richard's skills and talents for years. The only reason he'd insisted Richard mount up this morning was to get back at him for the embarrassment of being confronted by Max Jordan a few nights earlier.

It would do no good to complain about it now. He didn't want to give Grady the satisfaction of knowing he'd succeeded in making him miserable.

After they'd ridden for several minutes, they came to the holding-pen area. Laredo told him to dismount, then had him sort through the calves. It was his duty to separate the steers from the heifers. No easy task, and it irked Richard that his son-of-a-bitch brother-in-law took such delight in the trouble he had. Even the dog seemed to be working against him, instead of with him. Laredo was at the gate while Richard herded the cattle one way or the other. All too frequently, Laredo had to correct him, but then, Richard had never been any good with animals. He hated ranch life, and Grady knew it. His brother was unfairly trying to make him pay for circumstances beyond his control.

When they'd finished sorting the calves, they broke the steers into twenty-head lots and weighed them. Nothing hurt Richard's ears more than the sound of ill-tempered cattle thundering onto the scale. They weren't any more interested in being weighed than Richard was in finishing the task.

"Are they loaded?" Laredo shouted.

"Isn't it lunchtime yet?"

"No. Answer the question."

"They're on the scale," he shouted back, waving his hand in front of his face. Not only were cattle stupid and nasty, their stench gave him a headache.

Laredo did whatever he did with the controls of the scale and checked the balance. Richard watched it bob back and forth until the correct weight was found. Then the steers were moved into the holding pen.

Laredo seemed pleased with the results. "They've gained an average of fifty pounds in the past twenty days," he said.

"Whoopee."

Laredo ignored him. "At this rate they'll weigh around six hundred pounds by the sale date."

"Great," Richard muttered, seeing that his sarcasm was lost on the wrangler. He stared at his watch. "Isn't it lunchtime yet?"

"Soon." Laredo shoved back his hat with the heel of

one hand. "When we're finished here, Grady wants us to vaccinate the steers."

"*What?* You mean my brother actually expects me to give them shots? With a needle?"

"So it seems."

"I hate needles." Damn it, Laredo hadn't mentioned this earlier, and Richard just knew the omission had been on purpose. Probably figured he was saving the best for last, the bastard.

"I don't suppose the calves are fond of being vaccinated, either."

"Fine, then let's skip the entire procedure."

Laredo didn't bother to respond, and Richard accepted that there was no help for it. But down the line, his big brother was going to pay for the trouble and humiliation he'd caused. Oh, yes. Grady had learned about the bill with Max, but he didn't know about the others. Not yet. And by the time he *did* discover the amount of money Richard had charged...well, Richard would be long gone. Bye-bye Yellow Rose.

Who'd be smiling then? Who'd be feeling smug and superior? It was enough to carry Richard through the rest of the day.

ELLIE SPENT as much time as she could with Glen, but not nearly enough to satisfy either one of them. A September wedding date had been set, and she was busy making plans. At the moment Glen and his brother needed to get the herd to market; that was their immediate priority and not something Ellie could help with.

"I thought I'd find you in here," Glen said.

Ellie, who was in the sick pen with a couple of calves, smiled up at her fiancé. He wore his Stetson and cowhide chaps. His approach warmed her heart.

"Are these two going to make it?" she asked. Most calves had slick hair, bright eyes and big bellies, but the calves in the pen looked dull-eyed and thin.

"They don't have anything a little bit of medicine and some tender loving care won't cure."

"Good."

Glen joined her in the pen. "When did you get here?"

"Fifteen minutes ago. George is closing up this afternoon."

He kissed her briefly. "Thank him for me."

"He's going to have to get used to it. When we're married, I'll be leaving early sometimes."

Glen wrapped his arm around her waist. "I like the sound of that word."

"Married?"

He nodded, and opening the gate, ushered her out of the barn and toward the house. "I like the sound of it more and more every day."

"So do I," she admitted softly. And she thought to herself that her father would have liked the idea of his Ellie married. To her friend, who was his friend, too. She imagined him smiling, telling her she'd chosen well. John Frasier had liked Glen and respected him. Her only regret was that her father wouldn't be there to walk her down the aisle or dance at his daughter's wedding.

"Give me time to shower," Glen said as they entered the house. "I'll be back before you know it." He smiled down at her and then, as if he couldn't restrain himself, kissed her once again.

While Glen cleaned up, Ellie went into the kitchen to start dinner. Since they'd made their engagement official, she'd stopped by the ranch two or three nights a week. It only made sense for them to eat together. She'd taken a few cooking lessons from Dovie on preparing basic meals.

Meat and potatoes, mostly. Next thing, she'd tackle pies. She enjoyed practicing in the big ranch-house kitchen, especially with Glen there to cheer her on. Ellie found she begrudged every minute she couldn't spend with him, and she knew he felt the same way.

She had a roast in the oven and was peeling potatoes when Cal walked into the kitchen. "Hey, Ellie, how's it going?" he asked.

"Great," she said, dropping a freshly peeled potato into a kettle of water.

"You don't have to do this, you know. But let me tell you I appreciate every morsel."

Ellie grinned up at him. She was discovering that she liked Cal. Actually she always had, but he could be a difficult man to understand because he often seemed so remote, and sometimes even gruff. She'd been spending more time with him lately, and they'd developed a comfortable rapport. Ellie had even talked him into attending the Fourth of July celebration with her and Glen. To all appearances, he'd enjoyed himself, although he hadn't asked anyone to dance at the evening festivities. It was a well-known fact that he didn't trust women, although he was obviously pleased for her and Glen.

"You're welcome to join Glen and me for dinner any time after we're married," she told him. They'd already decided it would be most beneficial, considering her business, for Glen to move into town after the wedding and commute to the ranch every day. Soon they'd be setting up an appointment with a Realtor and looking at houses. Glen hoped to have the deal closed by August so that once they were married, they could move right in. Ellie hoped that was possible, too.

As soon as Glen reappeared, his hair wet and glistening from the shower, Cal quickly left the room. Glen's arms circled hers from behind and he kissed her neck. "Damn, but I love you."

Now that he was comfortable with the words, he said them often; he seemed to delight in sharing his feelings.

"I love you, too." The words had no sooner left her lips when she turned in his arms to face him. "I'm worried about Cal."

"Cal? What's wrong with my brother?"

"Nothing love wouldn't cure."

Glen frowned and took Ellie by the shoulders. "You've got that look in your eye. I've seen it in my mother's and Dovie Boyd's."

"What look?"

Glen kissed the tip of her nose. "I don't know what it's called, but it's what comes over a woman when she thinks she knows what's best for a man."

"I'm not trying to be a...a matchmaker, Glen!"

"But you think Cal needs a woman."

"He needs to fall in love."

"He did once," Glen reminded her.

"Next time it needs to be with a woman who'll love him just as much in return. Who'll appreciate him for who he is without trying to change him."

"And where do you intend to find such a woman?" Glen asked, his gaze holding hers.

"I don't know, but she's out there and just waiting for someone like Cal."

Glen eased Ellie back into his embrace and kissed her with a thoroughness that left no question about his own love for her. "You're a terrible romantic, Ellie Frasier-soon-to-be-Patterson."

"I'm a woman in love and I want my almost-brother-in-law to find happiness, too."

"He'll have to look for his own partner if he wants to do a Texas two-step."

Glen drew her closer still.

She smiled up at him. "Well," she said, "that's the thing about the two-step. There's no changing partners if you do it right." She raised her mouth to his in a teasing kiss.

"You can bet on that." And he kissed her back.

* * * * *

Come back to Promise next month! In CAROLINE'S CHILD you'll see how things develop between Grady and Caroline Daniels. Are they ever going to make a match of it—or not? And who is the father of Caroline's child? Visit newlyweds Savannah and Laredo and come to Glen and Ellie's wedding. See what Cal's up to. And Sheriff Frank Hennessey and Nell Bishop and everyone else...

MILLS & BOON®

Makes any time special

Copyright © Harlequin Enterprises I imited 1997
All rights reserved

Enjoy a romantic novel from Mills & Boon®

Presents™ *Enchanted*™ *Temptation*

Historical Romance™ *Medical Romance*™

MILLS & BOON®

Next Month's Romance Titles

♡

Each month you can choose from a wide variety of romance novels from Mills & Boon®. Below are the new titles to look out for next month from the Presents™ and Enchanted™ series.

Presents™

THE MARRIAGE DECIDER	Emma Darcy
TO BE A BRIDEGROOM	Carole Mortimer
HOT SURRENDER	Charlotte Lamb
THE BABY SECRET	Helen Brooks
A HUSBAND'S VENDETTA	Sara Wood
BABY DOWN UNDER	Ann Charlton
A RECKLESS SEDUCTION	Jayne Bauling
OCCUPATION: MILLIONAIRE	Alexandra Sellers

Enchanted™

A WEDDING WORTH WAITING FOR	Jessica Steele
CAROLINE'S CHILD	Debbie Macomber
SLEEPLESS NIGHTS	Anne Weale
ONE BRIDE DELIVERED	Jeanne Allan
A FUNNY THING HAPPENED…	Caroline Anderson
HAND-PICKED HUSBAND	Heather MacAllister
A MOST DETERMINED BACHELOR	Miriam Macgregor
INTRODUCING DADDY	Alaina Hawthorne

On sale from 5th March 1999

H1 9902

Available at most branches of WH Smith, Tesco, Asda, Martins, Borders, Easons, Volume One/James Thin and most good paperback bookshops

Enchanted™

★ SONS OF ★
PROMISE

DEBBIE MACOMBER

If you have enjoyed meeting the
characters in this book, look out for them
again next month in:

Caroline's Child

and again in:

April—Dr. Texas
May—Nell's Cowboy
June—Lone Star Baby

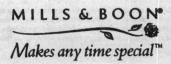

MILLS & BOON®

Makes any time special™

FREE!

4 Books
and a surprise gift!

We would like to take this opportunity to thank you for reading this Mills & Boon® book by offering you the chance to take FOUR more specially selected titles from the Enchanted™ series absolutely FREE! We're also making this offer to introduce you to the benefits of the Reader Service™—

★ FREE home delivery
★ FREE gifts and competitions
★ FREE monthly Newsletter
★ Books available before they're in the shops
★ Exclusive Reader Service discounts

Accepting these FREE books and gift places you under no obligation to buy; you may cancel at any time, even after receiving your free shipment. Simply complete your details below and return the entire page to the address below. *You don't even need a stamp!*

YES! Please send me 4 free Enchanted books and a surprise gift. I understand that unless you hear from me, I will receive 6 superb new titles every month for just £2.40 each, postage and packing free. I am under no obligation to purchase any books and may cancel my subscription at any time. The free books and gift will be mine to keep in any case.

N9EB

Ms/Mrs/Miss/Mr ....Initials ....
BLOCK CAPITALS PLEASE

Surname ....

Address ....

....

....Postcode ....

Send this whole page to:
THE READER SERVICE, FREEPOST CN81, CROYDON, CR9 3WZ
(Eire readers please send coupon to: P.O. BOX 4546, DUBLIN 24.)

Offer not valid to current Reader Service subscribers to this series. We reserve the right to refuse an application and applicants must be aged 18 years or over. Only one application per household. Terms and prices subject to change without notice. Offer expires 31st August 1999. As a result of this application, you may receive further offers from Harlequin Mills & Boon and other carefully selected companies. If you would prefer not to share in this opportunity please write to The Data Manager at the address above.

Mills & Boon Enchanted is a registered trademark owned by Harlequin Mills & Boon Limited.

The Drifter

SUSAN WIGGS

"Susan Wiggs turns an able and sensual hand to
the...story of the capable, strait-laced spinster
and sensual roving rogue."

—Publishers Weekly

MIRA® Available from 19th February 1999